Zombies
at
Tiffany's

To
Joseph,

love

Sam St...

x

ZOMBIES
AT
TIFFANY'S

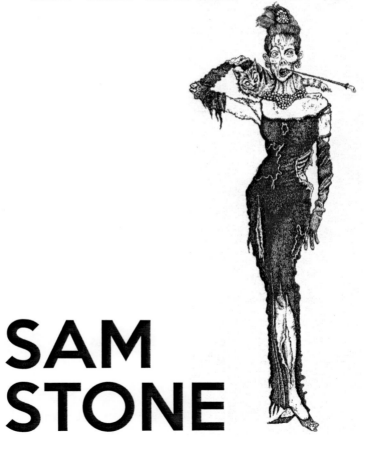

SAM
STONE

First published in England in 2012 by

Telos Publishing Ltd

17 Pendre Avenue, Prestatyn, Denbighshire, LL19 9SH

www.telos.co.uk

Telos Publishing Ltd values feedback. Please e-mail us with any comments you may have about this book to: feedback@telos.co.uk

ISBN: 978-1-84583-072-4 (paperback)

Zombies At Tiffany's © 2012 Sam Stone

Internal artwork © 2012 Russell Morgan

The moral right of the author has been asserted.

Typesetting by Arnold T Blumberg

www.atbpublishing.com

Printed by Berforts

British Library Cataloguing in Publication Data.

A catalogue record for this book is available from the British Library.

For Natasha and Leah

Prologue
The Darkness

Extracts From The Journal Of A Union Army Soldier

I floated in the happiness of ether as the doctor began to work on my leg. There was the numb, cold sensation – accompanied by a painless tugging – of running liquid as he poured whisky into the wound. I visualised him cutting into raw meat, felt the same indifference. Then I heard a *ping* as something was dropped into a small metal dish on the table beside me. He had removed the bullet. There was more tugging and a distant scraping as my thigh was roughly sewn up with catgut. I felt nothing.

It had hurt so much a short time ago. Now my limbs were heavy and numb. My chest heaved, my breathing was laboured. Shadows gathered around the tent like the spirits of the dead waiting to take me away to the next realm. I thought I would probably die. Can you understand that? Facing death?

My mind flashed back to the battlefield. The cries of war, the screams of the dying and the deafening retorts that echoed across the plain as soldiers fired their weapons: all were still ringing in my ears. The silence in the tent was torture. It made me feel less alive.

Yes. I was certain that death was nearby.

There was an oil lamp, and as the dark spread into the corners of my eyes, I felt the doctor move away, sensed the brightness intensify as he turned the lamp up, but my dulled vision could barely make out the canvas above my head.

I heard, rather than felt, a final splash of cleansing spirit over the now-sealed wound.

'George … you're going to be all right,' said the doctor. 'Rest now.'

The tent flaps opened as someone came in and the doctor stopped his work and glanced up.

'Is he going to make it, Doc?' asked a voice I knew. The Colonel, Jackson was his name, was making his rounds to see which of us were worth saving.

The doctor opened one of my eyelids with his thumb and gazed down as though he could see my soul.

'This one is fine. The wound was from a bullet, nothing else,' he said.

I drifted away. The ether darkness was all I knew

and it pulled me down into a deep, painless sleep. Even so, the dreams remained. The insanity of the day mixed around in my subconscious and the enemy became more monstrous than they really were.

It was full dark when I woke again. A dull ache throbbed through my thigh and pushed away the last traces of the anaesthetic.

The camp was quiet, as it should be, but my heart began to race as though I were an animal hiding from a predator. I remembered how I came to be here. The surgery, the ether. My throat was dry and a strange metallic taste was in my mouth. My head hurt and I felt sickness tugging at the insides of my stomach. *Had I lost my leg?* I wanted to see but I was afraid to look. I moved my heavy arms, tried to move my legs. Pain wracked through my thigh and hip. It felt as though it were still there, but I knew about phantom limbs, had seen many a soldier believe he was still whole when in fact parts of him were now scattered on the killing fields.

The flaps on the medical tent moved once more.

'I'm hungry …' said a voice. 'It's dark. So very dark …'

I tried to sit up, but my limbs were paralysed and I wasn't sure whether this was the after effects of the medication or whether fear had sapped my strength.

Something lurked in the doorway, as though waiting to be invited inside.

'What are you doing here?' demanded the doctor.

I turned my head and saw the doctor lying on another cot beside mine. He sat, pushing back the coarse grey blanket. My eyes followed him to the door of the tent.

'Doc … I'm hungry. Feed me …'

Somewhere there was light and the doctor's face was ashen in the pale glow that came from the camp outside. I imagined that the lamps were lit to scare away evil. I didn't know why this thought came to me, or why my heart continued to pump blood into my ears, deafening me with my own heartbeat as the doctor conversed calmly with the stranger at the entrance to the tent.

'You need to go and sleep this off,' the doctor said.

'I can't, Doc. It *bit* me.'

'In the morning you'll feel better.'

I raised my head and saw burning embers in the stranger's eyes and realised that it was Colonel Jackson. I wondered what had happened to him. He was usually so in control. But this man … he was troubled, pulled by more than lack of sleep and the pressure of command. He was haunted.

'I can give you something to help you sleep,' said the doctor.

'Yes,' said Jackson. 'Sleep. I need sleep.'

They left then, walking away. The tent flaps fell back in place. I was alone once more. I didn't like it, but the terror left my limbs and I was able to pull myself up into a seated position. I glanced down at the blanket covering my legs. In the gloom I could make out the shape of both of them, still there, still intact. Still whole. *Thank God.*

I sighed deeply and realised that I had been holding my breath. The leg – my thigh – ached but still I swung it over the side of the cot, wincing at the pain, but not allowing it to stop me. *Could I walk?*

I stood tentatively, taking the weight on my good leg first before testing the other one. Shooting pain pierced my hip. I leaned against the cot, gritting my teeth and hopping to relieve the discomfort.

My leg worked but it couldn't take weight. It hurt like the Devil when I tried. I looked around the tent for something that would make a crutch of some sort, and then I saw my walking stick, strangely and conveniently resting beside my trunk. The stick had been my grandfather's and I had brought it with me for luck. I noted with some consternation that everything I owned was now in this tent; my trunk, rucksack and my weapons all lay a few feet away from my cot. I hopped over to the trunk and I reached for the stick where it lay on top. I had always liked the big silver cat's head that crowned the wooden stick: mouth open; fangs bared like a roaring lion. It reminded me of the cats my grandfather had kept and loved for most of his life.

I slowly put my foot down, but rested my weight on the stick. The pain was bearable. Just. And so I hobbled to the door and looked out at the camp.

The light I had seen wasn't from oil lamps as I had first thought. There was a full moon and it shone down on the camp, lighting it up like a beacon with crisp white moonlight.

I saw a soldier walking the perimeter while another prodded a fire and added more sticks and leaves to keep it burning. Other than these two men there was no activity. I was just about to close the flap and return to my bed when I saw the doctor come out of Jackson's tent. He was staggering, holding his hand to his throat. His skin reflected the yellow of the camp fire and the white of the moon.

'Help him!' I called, stumbling forward out of the tent. I almost lost my footing as the cane slipped in the muddy, trampled earth.

The soldier tending the fire hurried to his aid, but as he approached I saw something happen that I couldn't explain. The doctor *changed*. He grabbed hold of the soldier, pulling him towards his open mouth. The moonlight illuminated his yellowed, slime-covered teeth seconds before the soldier pulled his handgun from his holster, pressed it to the doctor's temple and fired.

The doctor's legs crumpled, useless beneath him, and he fell to the floor at the feet of the now near-hysterical soldier.

'He was one of *them*!' he yelled.

The camp was in uproar as many of the soldiers rushed from their tents, rifles at the ready. They surrounded the dead doctor and the soldier.

'Did he bite you?' someone asked, but all the soldier

could do was shake his head. He was clearly in a state of total shock.

The Colonel lifted the flap of his tent. He came out into the light and I saw the same yellowed skin, hungry, burning eyes and foul teeth that had been the main features in the doctor's metamorphosis. His mouth and chin were covered with blood. I knew then that it was he who had bitten the doctor.

'Come to me boys,' he said. 'The darkness awaits you. Let it into your soul.'

I moved back into the tent as the Colonel stepped forward. All of the soldiers, barring the one that had shot the doctor, raised their rifles and aimed them at the Colonel.

The Colonel smiled. Saliva dripped from his polluted teeth. The soldiers fired.

The Colonel jumped forward, a crazed and hungry roar on his lips. He caught hold of a young cadet and clamped his mouth over the boy's right eye. The boy screamed, I heard a sickening pop, and the rest of the camp fell on both the Colonel and the boy.

They parted them. A black, bleeding hole remained where the soldier's eye had been. The Colonel had somehow sucked it right from the socket. The boy fell back, mouth open and slack with shock, and was caught by two other soldiers and dragged across the camp to be laid down by the camp fire. In the meantime, three men tried to restrain the Colonel, but they were all afraid of his snapping jaws.

'Don't let him bite you!' someone called.

The three men let go simultaneously and fell back as the soldiers fired at the Colonel. His body jerked, raised up by the impact, and he fell against his tent. The canvas ripped and the tent collapsed, covering the Colonel as he fell to the ground.

'Shoot!' called the Captain. The men let rip into the tent and I saw the Colonel's body jerk underneath the canvas.

They focused their efforts on his head. The bullets ripped into the canvas, pounding his skull into the ground. Blood seeped through the fabric, but the soldiers didn't stop firing until the body of the Colonel stopped moving and nothing more than a bloody pulp remained.

It was then that the injured boy by the camp fire sat up.

From my vantage point just inside the medical tent, I was the first to notice him moving. He turned his head and stared at me, and my eyes focused on the bloody hole rather than his remaining eye. A dull flame, some kind of inner evil, burned behind the empty socket.

My voice choked in my throat as I tried to raise the alarm. But the boy didn't come for me as I expected. Instead he stood and turned and walked out of the camp.

I collapsed to my knees, the pain in my thigh intensified and I felt I had looked death once more in the eye. Could I ever be lucky a third time?

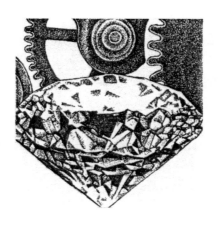

One

It was the summer of 1862 when I started my new job. My brother, Henry, had gone away to join the Union Army to fight against the Confederates leaving my young sister Sally and me with our mother. At the time, Mother was taking in sewing work – she had been among the first to invest in a Singer machine – but the meagre pittance she earned for hours and hours of backbreaking effort was barely enough to pay back the hire-purchase on the machine, let alone cover all of our other living costs. I was 18 when I found myself to be the main breadwinner in our family.

It was a strange time. Women weren't really thought of as the workforce in New York, yet suddenly, with the ever-decreasing male population who were leaving to sign up in the Federal Army, we were left with little choice but to support ourselves and find the best work we could.

Most went on to factory work, or became waitresses in tea rooms and bars, while others, like me, found their employment in the still thriving centre of the grid that constituted New York.

I was luckier than most. I landed a prime job at Tiffany and Co on Fifth Avenue in Lower Manhattan.

It felt like an adventure going to work. I was good with figures and well turned out; it was what made me stand out in the sea of applicants who applied for the job of sales assistant.

That first morning I donned my uniform: an austere black skirt, high-necked white blouse, and a formal fitted day jacket that matched the skirt. Underneath the long skirt I wore my most comfortable walking shoes. I was wearing a corset too, but mother had fastened it loosely, even though by then I was quite used to wearing them. Shop rules stated that all the female assistants had to wear their hair swept up and away from their face. I'd never worn mine so formally before and I marvelled at how sophisticated I looked as Sally and Mother put in the last pins and my hair was held securely high on top of my head.

'That should hold,' said Mother, adding a final pin for good measure.

There was no point in complaining though; to do so would have brought forth a lecture that I'd learnt by heart. *Kat, you have a responsibility to this family now. You're the eldest. What would happen to Sally if you don't go to work? Be sensible, do as you're told and bring home your pay every Friday.* Mother's lecture was unnecessary, however. I wanted to work and the opportunity that Tiffany's afforded meant more to me than the continuing education my family had originally planned.

'There!' said Mother, finally satisfied.

I stared at my reflection. My full, wavy, black hair was now tamed and the uniform, as severe as it was, made me look grown up. Mother handed me her best paste brooch. It contained amber and red glass and it looked like real precious stones, even though we all knew it wasn't. I fastened it on the blouse at my throat and I stood up and stepped back from the dresser to survey my look.

'My word!' Mother said. 'You look so …'

'You look like a married lady,' Sally piped up. She was 11 and had the habit of saying whatever popped into her head. Mother often chose to ignore it, but I was sure that Sally was so outspoken because no-one ever told her not to be.

'Very sophisticated, I was going to say,' said Mother.

I lifted the black jacket from the back of the chair and slipped it on, quickly buttoning it. My bosom was accentuated by the way the coat fitted, because it buttoned up to just underneath. I turned around, looking at the back of the skirt. The bustle was small, a little old hat by Paris fashion, but modesty was the key thing about the uniform.

'Ready?' asked Mother.

'Yes,' I said.

'Then you had better get going, you don't want to be late your first day,' she said, placing a small package in my hand, wrapped up with string. I stared at the package blankly.

'Your lunch, dear,' said Mother.

'Of course!'

The shop and building of Tiffany's was a 20 minute walk from our small townhouse. It was a bright morning and the streets were very quiet. I realised I had never been out on my own this early before. The streets of New York City felt safe to me though. This was my home, the place I'd grown up.

As I walked down the street I saw the milk cart driving slowly towards the row of townhouses. As always the farmer, Mr Berry, was on time with his huge metal cans full of fresh milk and cream. He waved to me as he went by, and I smiled and waved back.

At the end of the street I saw a grime-covered urchin throwing stones onto the road as he sat on the sidewalk. His head was downcast, and he looked miserable. He was wearing a ragged brown jacket and shorts. I noticed how thin his legs were and took pity on him. I opened my lunch pack and held out a chunk of bread. He looked up at me, at first suspiciously. Then, when his hunger pushed aside the fear, he reached out and took the bread from my hand.

'Thanks, Miss,' he said, and rapidly set about eating it.

In the next street a row of horse-drawn carriages lined up on the cobbled surface. These were cabs and they were waiting for their early morning fares. One of the drivers tipped his hat as I passed and I nodded back but hurried on, because I wasn't sure that to talk to him would have been very proper.

I arrived at the store at eight and the streets were rapidly filling up with workers, commuters and shoppers.

At the trade entrance, the security guard surveyed me with disdain.

'What's your name?' he asked rudely.

'Miss Lightfoot. Katherine Lightfoot.'

The guard looked at his list and frowned. 'I don't see you on my list.'

'I'm a new employee. Mr Levy, the manager, interviewed me last week. See, I even have the uniform ...'

The guard took in my uniform and nodded. 'You'll have to wait here.'

The guard closed the door and I waited outside feeling somewhat like a criminal. I noted that there was a metal grille lying open against the wall and it crossed my mind that this was for added security for the shop. It also reminded me that I was in the back alley, not a place I was keen to loiter for long. I let my mind drift away from the unease I was feeling and thought about the guard instead. He was in his late thirties. I wondered why he hadn't joined the war effort with most of the other men under 40.

Just then the trade entrance door creaked open and a young, attractive woman smiled at me. She was taller than me and a little thinner, with pale blonde wispy hair, which was also scraped back in the severe bun we had been told to wear. I guessed that she must have been about 25, but I didn't like to ask, because Mother had always taught me that it was rude to ask people's ages.

'You must be Katherine. I'm Sylvia. Come in and don't mind Edward, he likes to throw his weight around because he got rejected when he tried to sign up.'

'Call me Kat,' I said. 'Why was he turned down?'

'He can't see farther than his hands. It would be dangerous putting a weapon in them.'

I followed Sylvia inside as she told me more about Edward Brewster. He had been the security guard at Tiffany's for some time now. I learnt that he was married with three children and his aging mother lived with them. Why this was all relevant I couldn't guess, but it was clear Sylvia liked to gossip.

'He's a little hen-pecked at home,' she smiled. 'It's why he likes to seem so tough at work.'

Through the first door into the building I found myself in a small reception area. Edward had his own table and a chair and he returned to sit down at it. He made me smile, because he was attempting to look so official as he shuffled his list around on the desk, a snub-nosed pencil behind his ear.

'This way,' said Sylvia and I followed her through another door. This one led into a wide corridor that had several doors coming off it.

The first door was open.

'This is our kitchen,' Sylvia explained. 'Did you remember to bring something for lunch?'

I lifted my arm, showing my reticule, which contained the packed lunch Mother had given me.

I looked around the room. There was a heavy table in the corner, a deep sink, several chairs, and a cupboard stacked up with cups and saucers and a large teapot. Towards the back of the room was a large fireplace with a stove and a blackened kettle. On the wall nearest the door was a cabinet with several doors, each with a small padlock holding it closed.

'These are the lockers. You can store your lunch and anything else you have here. We're not allowed to take our purses out on the shop floor.'

Sylvia gave me a key and pointed to a small locker with a name tag on it. I noticed that she wasn't wearing a wedding ring, which was somewhat unusual for an attractive women of her age. The tag on the locker said 'MARGARET', but Sylvia pulled it off and replaced it with another one. She took a piece of charcoal from the pocket of her skirt and paused, looking at me.

'Ah,' I realised. 'Kat. With a K.'

Sylvia wrote 'KAT' on the new tag.

'There. Now everyone knows this is yours.'

I found this to be a rather strange practice, but thanked her anyway.

'Now, other things you should know. Some of the girls from the workshop come in here too. They are a little peculiar about having their own chairs, so if you use this one …' – Sylvia pointed to a small stool in the corner of the room, next to a roughly carved wooden kitchen table – 'then you won't upset anyone, because that was Margaret's.'

'Oh. Right. What happened to Margaret?' I asked, certain that she would enjoy telling me.

Sylvia stared at me. 'We don't ask awkward questions around here if we want to keep our jobs. Margaret left. That's all you need to know.'

'Oh. Sorry … I didn't mean …'

I stowed my jacket and packed lunch in the small locker and followed Sylvia out into the corridor. I was frowning a little because I was concerned that I had upset her, but I soon found that Sylvia was a contrary character. One minute she would gossip, but when questioned, she often took the moral high ground and refused to answer. I think it was because she liked people to think she knew more about what was happening at Tiffany's than she actually did.

'Down to the right are the male and female washrooms. At the end of the corridor to the right are the stairs that go up to the first floor. That is where the work rooms are. And here,' she paused at a door on the left, 'is the shop floor.'

The door was closed and Sylvia explained that it should be kept closed at all times. I noticed two heavy bolts that ran across the top and bottom of the door – currently open – and a mortice lock in the centre near the handle.

'During the day this is unlocked, but in the evening the bolts are drawn and the lock engaged,' said Sylvia. Then she opened the door and I followed her inside.

On the shop floor we met Mr Gerald Levy, who I also thought was an odd character. Levy was the manager at Tiffany's, and at that time I never saw the owner, but the other workers commented frequently on how nice Mr Charles was.

I had seen the interior of the shop before, as I had visited it with Mother when we were looking for a crucifix for Sally's last birthday. It was set out unlike most stores of the time. Tiffany's had a price transparency policy and all of their jewellery was labelled clearly with a price. These items were displayed on velvet-covered trays in glass-topped cabinets. The cabinets lined the walls with just enough room behind for Sylvia, Levy and me to move around the room. The rest of the floor was open and carpeted and it allowed the customers room to move freely around and observe what was in the locked cases. There was also an impressive and ornate grandfather clock behind the table containing the till, and it marked time loudly, chiming with grand peals every hour.

Levy gave me a set of keys for the cabinets so that I could open them to show items to customers, but I was always to keep them tied to my belt, and in the evenings I had to give them back to Levy to lock away for the night.

During my initial interview I had observed that Levy was attractive for an older man. He must have been at least 40 at the time, but he had a shock of thick, black, wavy hair that he slicked back with some kind of shiny cream. He wore smart and expensive suits, with chic cravats made from French silk, which showed that he must be well paid in his role as manager of such an expensive store. Levy was Jewish. This wasn't obvious in any way except for when he became excited and forgot to speak formally to us. At those times he began to spout Yiddish.

'Our silverware is renowned,' Levy told me that first day. 'Do you know, Miss Lightfoot, that Tiffany's are supporting the Union Army?'

I didn't reply. I had quickly learnt that when Levy began to talk of patriotism you didn't interrupt him. He was living the American dream and he believed in the country like all immigrants did in those days. No-one judged him for his faith, in fact Jews were hard-working citizens and Levy was a testament to how anyone could be successful.

'We have been providing swords and most importantly we have made special surgical tools for the battlefield surgeons,' he continued with pride in his voice.

I blinked at this. We hadn't heard from my brother for months; the thought that he might be injured didn't sit well with me. I did hope that Henry would return from the war unscathed and heroic, just as Mother always portrayed him.

'Our heroes need us! That's why we must behave with dignity and not like a load of *meshugginas* …'

'That means insane people,' murmured Sylvia translating Levy's Yiddish for me when he had disappeared into the back. 'He *always* uses that one … You'll get used to it.'

Tiffany's employees were a small, exclusive family to which I quickly belonged. I settled in my new role, rapidly learning the ropes and patiently dealing with customers, wealthy and poor alike, I also learnt that my employers did other things as well as provide jewellery and trinkets.

On the shop floor, Sylvia and I worked mostly alone with Levy, but often Martin Crewe was brought down from his workshop on the second floor. Martin was the designer. As well as guiding the jewellers, he was a wonderfully talented clockmaker. He created the most beautiful and intricate pocket watches.

'See this,' he told me as he carefully opened the back of his latest design. 'It has a double movement.'

'Sorry Martin, I don't know what that means,' I said.

'The clock is self winding: as one movement works it winds the other, then it switches and the process is reversed.'

'You don't have to wind up the watch?' I asked.

'Never.'

'That's really clever!' I said, and I was impressed.

I learnt that Martin was from a long line of watchmakers. His father, Crichton Crewe, had worked for the original owner way back when Tiffany's first opened its doors in 1837. Martin was a little bit of a rebel though. He was talented but he liked to design his own things. Some of which were to come in very handy over the next few months.

'Of course he should have been drafted,' Sylvia said, 'but Mr Charles pulled a few strings and Martin remained. Tiffany's couldn't run without him, you see. He designs everything here.'

At that moment the shop door opened and the first customers of the day came in. I couldn't question Sylvia more about Martin or Mr Charles as the daily rush began.

'You girl,' said Lady Barclay. 'Pull out that tray of rings and let me see them.' She held up her spectacles on their gold stalk. By then I could recognise the handiwork of the Tiffany's jewellers and the hallmarks that gave the gold such distinction. I reached into the counter and pulled the tray up, and Lady Barclay spent the next hour trying on rings until she finally chose an ostentatious diamond and ruby setting, which she placed on her pudgy middle finger. Her husband dutifully paid for it: the ring cost more than I would earn in a year.

Afterwards a young couple came in to buy an

engagement ring. They couldn't afford real diamonds, so I led them over to the gemstones.

'This is beautiful, Freddie,' said the girl. She was a pretty young thing with shiny red hair and a warm smile that Freddie clearly loved.

I retrieved the amber ring from the tray and placed it before her. Freddie frowned when he saw the price tag.

'Just a minute,' I said lifting up the tray next to it. This contained some of the store's finest costume jewellery and it was a fraction of the price, even though to the naked eye it looked almost as good.

The bride-to-be clapped her hands in delight as I gave her a silver setting that contained a near-perfect glass jewel that looked just like a real sapphire.

'I think silver is so much nicer than gold,' I said to the girl. 'Please try it on.'

The ring looked as elegant as I had hoped it would, and Freddie was happy with the price. He paid and the couple left. I watched them through the shop window as they walked down Fifth Avenue. The future bride was holding out her hand and constantly admiring the expensive-looking ring.

'Another happy customer!' said Levy behind me. 'You really are very good at this, Miss Lightfoot.'

'Thank you, Mr Levy,' I said.

I turned back to look around the shop and saw Sylvia frowning at us from behind the counter. I raised my eyebrow at her and formed the question on my face but

Sylvia's cheeks reddened and she looked away. Then she began to bustle around the now empty shop, tidying trays and polishing the glass on the counter tops. I hurried to help her, but she was unusually quiet for the rest of the afternoon.

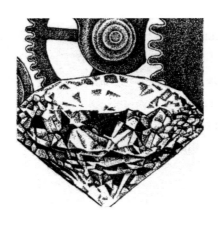

Two

'Miss Lightfoot,' Martin said as I was stowing my jacket and reticule in my locker. 'Mr Levy told me to show you the way to the work room this morning. I'm to give you a tour of the production process. Apparently it will help you sell, and I quote, "exclusive jewellery designs to our more affluent customers".'

I was often in work early and, other than Edward, Martin was always in too. He was also the last to leave at night and I did begin to wonder if he in fact lived in one of the rooms on the upper levels that I hadn't seen. I didn't like to ask Sylvia though. She obviously hated to be questioned, even though she frequently told me things without prompting. I knew it would be just a matter of time before she told me all she knew about Martin … but it always had to be on her terms.

Martin Crewe had intrigued me from the start. It was

difficult to determine his age, but I thought he might be around 27. To say Martin was unusual would have been an understatement. He was in fact very eccentric, and for such a young man he had something of the 'mad professor' about him. I found him attractive though, because he was so highly intelligent and so very interesting compared with other people I had met.

I followed Martin down the corridor, past the washrooms, to the stairs on the right. At the top of the stairs was a door that Martin opened, and it led into a large workroom. The room took up half of the floor space, and I learnt it was the jewellery design and construction area.

I looked around and saw three sets of tables and benches with trays of silver and gold rings and necklaces in various stages of being manufactured. There was a huge drawing on a working easel of an ornate tiara that showed a setting containing over a hundred diamonds.

'That's beautiful,' I said, admiring the workmanship.

Martin shrugged. 'I do the sketches so large so that the makers can see all of the detail required.'

Martin unlocked a cupboard that held a tray with the tiara frame already made in gold. It looked like the laurel leaf crowns I had seen goddesses wear in a book I had of classical mythology. Some of the diamonds were already set in the piece and I could already tell how magnificent the headdress was going to be.

'This was commissioned. And so you can see the

design concept to the semi-finish.'

I glanced down into the tray holding the tiara and saw the diamonds scattered in the bottom on green felt. They glowed like drops of morning dew on leaves.

'Exactly one hundred,' said Martin. 'All cut to perfect accuracy.'

'But how? How can you get them all the same?' I asked.

'It takes practice, and I have to admit that not all of them turn out well.' Martin slid the tray back into the cupboard and then pulled out another beneath it. 'Off-cuts.'

I glanced down at a sea of diamond chips that almost filled the tray.

'I suppose these aren't of any use now?' I asked.

Martin was silent for a moment. 'Sometimes we can salvage bits of these for the cheaper jewellery. Small diamond settings ... I'm sure you've see those.'

I nodded.

'But I have another use for them. One that is far more ...'

'Ah! There you are Kat,' said Sylvia from the doorway. I had been so engrossed in Martin's diamonds that I hadn't heard her light tread on the bare wooden stairs. 'Time to open up. You can finish the tour on your break time.'

'Thank you, Mr Crewe,' I said.

'Just call me Martin,' he answered. 'Everyone else

does and we don't stand on formality here.'

I nodded. Then turned to leave after making a final sweep of the room with my eyes. I noticed another door at the back and wondered if this led to Martin's living quarters. I was also curious to note that I couldn't see any stairs that led up to the next three floors. Tiffany's, from the outside, was five storeys high.

I left the room as Martin stowed the diamonds back in his cupboard, and as I followed Sylvia downstairs my mind was full of the off-cut diamonds. In their rugged way, they were far more beautiful than the set, perfect stones.

A few hours later I had the opportunity to go back to the workshop. Lady Elsie Beaufort had arrived with Major Thadeus Tinker, and she wanted to collect a necklace that had been designed for her.

Martin wasn't there when I entered the workshop. The girls I occasionally saw making tea in the back room, or eating their meagre lunches, were working solidly, heads down, making the designs that Martin had given them.

'I've come to collect Lady Elsie's necklace,' I said to no-one in particular. The girls ignored me, but I heard the sounds of machinery and looked towards the other door that I had noticed across the room. I walked through the workshop. None of the girls raised their heads, so I opened the door to the other room, looking for Martin.

I found him operating a strange gadget. He was turning the handle of what looked like a Singer sewing machine much like the one Mother owned, but it had been adapted and changed. There were new parts of metal added to it. A long barrel that looked as though it had been harvested from a rifle was inserted in the top. Two more barrels ran down where the arm was, and what had once been the foot, containing the needle with which you could sew material together, was a blunt piece of metal that moved up and down and around a diamond. There was a bright light shining down on the diamond, and Martin was wearing dark glasses as he looked at the stone through a magnifying glass.

'What is that?' I asked.

Martin jumped, 'What are you doing in here?'

'I came to get Lady Elsie's necklace.'

'You should ask one of the girls then. No-one is allowed in here.'

I looked around the room and found it was full of weird and wonderful machines. Something that resembled a musket was lying on a table top surrounded by bits of metal.

'That's a Springfield Model 1861 Rifled Musket,' Martin said when he saw my interest. 'I'm adapting it.'

'Adapting?' I said. 'But that's the latest thing. I think my brother Henry had …'

'Look,' said Martin, interrupting me and picking up the musket. 'It's so limited. Every time a soldier fires he has to reload. What I'm working on is something that will automatically load the bullet and the gunpowder.'

I nodded, but then my attention was drawn to a sword that rested on a stand as though for display only.

'This is beautiful,' I said. It had a shiny silver pommel and the same distinctive hallmark that all of Martin's work had. I reached out towards the polished surface.

'Don't touch it!' Martin warned, and I pulled my hand back quickly.

'It's been sharpened with dialight. That sword can cut through bone. It could sever someone's head without much of a swing.'

'What do you mean sharpened by dialight?' I asked.

'Can you keep a secret?'

I nodded.

'Come back later and I'll explain what I'm doing.'

I left his workroom, but not before I noticed yet another door at the bottom on the right. I wondered if this led upstairs, and I admit felt a little more curious than I had done about the rest of the floors in the store.

'Your necklace, Lady Elsie,' Levy said with a flourish as I held out the jewellery on a tray covered with black velvet.

'Splendid! I must try it on.'

I helped Lady Elsie fasten the clasp and hurried to fetch a mirror for her to see the necklace. The diamonds and emeralds rested against her bosom over a sheen of pale green taffeta, but I was sure the effect was no less impressive than it would be when she wore the necklace later that month at the Major's annual ball. No doubt then

Lady Elsie's outfit would be something magnificent. She certainly had style. As I returned with the mirror, I saw her take a quick and surreptitious swig from a silver flask with an emerald top. The emerald matched the jewels on the necklace perfectly, and I wondered if this too had been designed by Martin for her.

'What do you think, Major?' Lady Elsie asked, dropping the flask discretely into her reticule.

'Utterly splendid, my dear. You will be the belle of the ball.'

I placed the necklace in a box and carefully wrapped it. Then I held it out to Lady Elsie and she placed it in her reticule alongside the flask as Levy wrung his hands together, waiting for the final payment.

Major Tinker rubbed his mutton-chop whiskers as he reviewed the bill. 'She's worth every penny,' he said.

'Gin,' whispered Sylvia in my ear.

'What?'

'In her flask. It's her favourite tipple.'

'How do you know?'

'Mr Levy told me. The Major turns a blind eye to it because he is utterly devoted to her.' Sylvia sighed. 'Isn't that romantic?'

I knew nothing about romance and so didn't answer.

Soon after that, when there was a lull in the shop, I took a break and hurried straight back upstairs to see more of Martin's gadgets.

As I re-entered the workroom, the benches and stools

were empty, and I realised that the girls were all on their break too.

'Martin?' I called.

'In here.'

I went back into Martin's workroom and found some new things had been put out, presumably for me to see. There was a handgun lying on the table.

'This is a Remington 1858.' Martin proceeded to load the gun with what he explained was a cylinder magazine. It was a speed loader and it had given Martin an idea.

'The loader is removable,' he said, 'which means that I could substitute it with a different loader and, more importantly, different bullets.'

Then Martin showed me the loader and bullets he had designed. Although it looked the same at first glance, I soon learned that this loader took a very different kind of bullet. Although the bullet casing was identical to the original, the projectile head – the part that was fired out of the gun by the ignition of the gunpowder in the casing – was filled with diamond off-cuts. These special bullets were loaded by the handful into the empty magazine, which had been adapted to take double the amount of ammunition. That was because it was an extra cylinder that attached to the original, giving it double capacity. The two cylinders rolled together, turning each other like engine cogs.

'But Martin, the bullets have diamond shards inside them,' I pointed out. 'How can that work?'

'Believe me, diamonds are the toughest substance in the world. These will stop the enemy just as easily as a traditional bullet. Especially if you aim well. You see, when the bullet enters through the skin, it crumples, releasing all of the diamond shards, which then fly out into the body. That can do an awful lot of damage to your enemy.'

I grimaced. I didn't understand why Martin wanted to create weapons. It was a strange pastime, but at least I knew some of his technology went to the war effort and might someday save my brother's life.

'How had you adapted the sewing machine?' I asked, changing the subject.

'Ah – now that is my pride and joy. This is my dialight. It's how I'm cutting diamonds these days.'

Martin explained the process of using his dialight, and how the diamonds themselves created energy. He pointed to the top barrel and I noticed that it had a small hole cut in a rectangle. There was a tiny mirror on hinges that he moved in various ways. It was, it seemed, how he trapped the light inside. The light then travelled down into the barrel and out over the diamond below.

I decided that Martin was far more interesting than he was eccentric. He was certain that one day his weapons and inventions would be used to save lives. I unfortunately could see only how they could take and destroy lives. Even so, Martin was a fascinating man and I knew I wanted to see more of his extraordinary inventions in action.

Three

The cat appeared a few weeks later.

I was cleaning out the stockroom just off the shop floor. This was where we kept duplicate sizes of rings, and the stocks of costume jewellery that we didn't want to sell direct from the display cases. That day we had been extremely busy and the stock shelves were untidy. Sylvia pulled rank and stayed to do the nicer job of straightening the shop, but I didn't mind organising the stockroom. It gave me time alone with my thoughts, and it was a peaceful way to end the day.

I did have rather a lot to think about.

It had been so busy that I had been able to snatch only a few moments break, during which I had quickly eaten a hunk of cheese and bread from my lunch pack. So, I paused in my work. Then I remembered the letter. I reached into my skirt pocket and pulled out the envelope that Mother had received the day before. The paper was creased and I smoothed it out and immediately recognised the lovely neat handwriting: Henry was doing well, it seemed.

Dear Mother, Kat and Sally,

I am writing to let you know that I am well.

Colonel Kendal has taken rather a shine to me and so I have been assigned as his assistant. I can't say much about the war effort for security reasons but rest assured we are going to win this fight and those god-awful Southerners will be pushed back into the pit they crawled out of.

I'm sure you've heard the rumours that we soldiers are having a rough time of it.

Let me put your minds at rest. War is never a pleasant thing but we mustn't grumble at our lot. We eat regularly, Mother, so please don't worry. A soldier's life is to serve his country and we are all doing that the best way we can.

Colonel Kendal has promised our troop some furlough soon. And, when the relief arrives I'm sure to be able to come home again for some brief respite.

I hope you are all well. I haven't received any letters from you, but then the mail here is erratic so please don't worry if I don't get to reply to anything you've sent.

How are you, Kat? I was wondering and worrying, I must admit, if you did manage to find work to help out at home? As a private I only receive $13 a month, but I've arranged to have some of this sent to mother. It isn't much but it will help, I'm sure.

Mother, I hope your health is improved and that Sally isn't being too loud and annoying at the moment. Sorry Sal, but you can be very, very loud!

Well that's all I have time for now. The Colonel is calling for me and I have duties to attend to.

Much Love
Henry

I felt heartened by Henry's note as I pushed it back into my pocket. My thoughts were full of the reply I would send him. I had so much to tell him about Tiffany's and I was excited that the job had brought me to such a profoundly unusual friendship with Martin. Then I remembered that Martin had sworn me to secrecy about his weapons and his dialight machine. *Damn! I would so have loved sharing that with Henry. He'd be fascinated too!*

I pushed the thought of confiding in Henry away and continued to straighten the stockroom. A few minutes later I heard a small sound. It was a soft cry, not unlike that of a baby, and it was coming from one of the doors behind me.

I listened at the diamond stock cupboard door. This one was locked, and the key was on Mr Levy's key-ring. We had to have permission to open and take the jewellery from this area, and I had never had reason to ask before. I heard the gentle mewling sound again, so I went back into the shop to look for Mr Levy.

The shop was closed, the door locked and the shutters down. The outside world could not see inside, but I could see the room, and I found Sylvia and Levy embracing. I stepped back into the stockroom, realising that they had forgotten I was there.

'Gerald, you promised you would leave her ...' Sylvia said.

'What do you want already? I give you everything.'

'I want a wedding band, Gerald. You *promised*.'

'I don't think you appreciate how difficult it is for a Jew to leave his wife ... *Oy vey ...*'

I was shocked at what I heard and shrank back further into the stockroom, hoping they wouldn't notice I had seen them. I could hear Levy begin to kiss Sylvia and I felt my cheeks burn in much the same way hers had when Levy complimented me, except now I understood why she had been quiet and upset by that. She was worried that Levy was interested in me. Had I known about their relationship I would have reassured her. Levy was not my type, and my mother brought me up right. I just wasn't that kind of girl. I would never get involved with a married man. This thought raised the question in my mind of what type of girl this actually made Sylvia. I didn't want to think of her private life, it wasn't in any of our discussions, and now I knew why. Sylvia and Levy were having an affair, and Levy was married. This was not good knowledge to have.

The kissing outside intensified. I became concerned about how far this was all going to go. At some point my presence would have to become known; after all it was almost home time and Levy would want to lock up. As it was, the workshop had closed, the jewellers gone home, with the exception of Martin, who I now knew often stayed late to work on his other projects.

I turned around and continued straightening the shelves and cupboards, making as much noise as I could to drown out the sounds in the shop, and I hoped that they would hear me and remember I was there. My ploy worked. A few minutes later, Sylvia popped her head around the door and looked in at me.

'All done?' she asked.

'Almost. I just need the key to this cupboard ...' I said.

Sylvia held out the thick bunch of keys that Levy always carried. 'Here you go. I have to leave now. Will you lock up?'

'Of course.'

Sylvia quickly showed me the right key. 'Edward is on the trade entrance and will let you out as usual. He's here until late today.'

I didn't question Sylvia, or the fact that she had Levy's keys, but I waited for them to leave before I opened the other door. I realised what a responsibility it was that I had been given the keys. Levy wasn't usually careless about these things, but I knew that I would never steal from the store, so I thought that maybe he knew it also.

Inside the closet I found another shelf unit containing the expensive jewellery, a huge safe built into the wall and a small black and white cat that was little more than a kitten.

'How did you get in here?' I asked, bobbing down as the tiny animal ran to my ankles and began to rub against the hem of my skirt.

I stroked the cat and it purred. 'You're really lovely but you can't stay in here.'

It was a mystery how the cat had gotten into the cupboard holding the safe, when this cupboard was always locked. I picked up the cat and snuggled it and then I closed the door and relocked it. I left the stockroom, also locking the door behind me. All of this made me even more aware of the impossibility of the animal finding its way accidently inside. But who would purposely lock some poor little creature away like that? *Maybe it was a surprise present for Sylvia from Levy*, I thought.

I had the cat and the bunch of keys but wasn't sure what to do with either of them as I stood in the shop. So I went back to the kitchen and opened my locker. I put the cat down while I pulled on my jacket and removed the reticule that I had carried my personal effects in that morning. Then I locked the keys in my locker for safe-keeping. I was afraid to take them home in case they were somehow mislaid.

The cat padded around me on the rough carpet and looked up at me. She meowed softly and I bent to pick her up again.

'What am I going to do with you?' I said. 'Do you have a name? I can't call you Cat, that's what everyone calls me.' I thought for a moment. 'You look like a Holly to me. I always liked that name, it reminds me of Christmas.'

The newly christened Holly meowed. She seemed to like the name too.

I opened my reticule and removed the remains of my lunch. Then I poured a little milk into a saucer and placed Holly down in front of it. She didn't seem too interested, but with a little encouragement the cat drank the semi-warm milk and I sat down in Sylvia's seat to watch her.

When the saucer was empty I washed it in the sink and I picked up Holly again.

'Well you can't stay here, so you're just going to have to come home with me,' I said finally.

I stowed her in my reticule. She purred contentedly. I didn't know it then but Holly was going to become an important part of my life.

Edward let me out into the weak daylight. I was leaving later than usual and the dullness in the alley made me feel a little uncomfortable. As I walked towards the main street I thought I heard something behind me.

ZOMBIES AT TIFFANY'S

I turned and glanced over my shoulder at the trash cans, pausing for a moment. There were dark shadows gathered around that area: like a thick dark fog. Inside my reticule Holly hissed and then I heard a small yowl as two cats appeared from nowhere. They stalked the shadowed area around the bins, sniffing and meowing, until I saw a man stagger out from behind the cans.

Both cats arched their backs and yowled. Holly wriggled inside my reticule.

I can't say that I felt comforted at all by the sight of this strange man. He was wearing what would have been an expensive suit if it hadn't been so torn and dirty, but he was wrong in so many other ways too. I noticed he was staring at me over the cats, his eyes held the strangest expression. As though there was something missing behind them. No thought. No emotion. No conscience. I don't know why, but all of these things popped into my head as I studied him.

He took a step forward but the presence of the cats seemed to worry him and so they should; they were obviously wild and vicious. One of the cats began to prowl closer to the man, just like a lion stalking its prey. He backed away again, eyes going from the animals then back to me, but there was no plea for help in them. There was something else, unfathomable and almost predatory.

My heart began to race and I hurried out of the alley into the main street, and the sound of screeching cats echoed in the air.

Four

I arrived home that evening to see a mover's cart outside of the townhouse next door. The owner, Mrs Handley, took in lodgers. It was the only way she could afford to live in these hard times and it had been something that Mother and I had talked about doing if I didn't find work. Fortunately we hadn't needed to open our doors to strangers. I hadn't cared for the idea at all, and neither had Mother.

Mrs Handley's new lodger was hefting a heavy bag up the front steps while the cart driver brought up a large trunk with the aid of his young assistant.

'Good day,' said the lodger.

I was already unnerved by what had happened as I had left work and so I bowed my head and scurried into the house. I wasn't sure Mother would care for me talking to someone I didn't know anyway. Even though I did that all day these days, it was different on the street, and the lodger, if he were a respectable man, should have known that. We hadn't been introduced and I wasn't that sort of girl. I thought about Sylvia and Levy and realised that Mother's snobbery would most certainly extend to their peculiar relationship. She would no doubt think it a great scandal. I decided I would never confide this information about my day at Tiffany's. It would be just the sort of thing that would set her off on a lecture, and she might even expect me to leave the job if she were outraged enough. I had no intention of leaving Tiffany's. My life had become far more interesting since I had begun to work there.

'Kat!' said Sally running up to me as I closed the front door. 'Mrs Handley has a lodger. He's a reporter and he's been covering the war in the newspapers.'

'Really?' I said.

'Yes. He's called George Pepper.'

'That's funny. I thought he looked like a *Henry* or a *Freddie* but not at all like a George,' I said.

'Have you seen him?' Sally said.

'Yes. Just now.'

'Was he handsome?'

'Sally, how on Earth would I know? It was very brief.'

'Did you speak to him?'

'Certainly not. We haven't been introduced.'

Mother came into the hallway and a lovely smell of roast ham wafted out of the kitchen. I placed my reticule down by the post at the bottom of the stairs and removed my jacket. I had almost completely forgotten about Holly inside until she gave a furious meow.

'Good heavens,' said Mother. 'What have you got in there?'

I opened the bag and Holly poked her shiny black head out to stare wide-eyed at Mother and Sally.

'Wow!' said Sally. 'A cat! Can we keep it?'

Mother pursed her lips but didn't say 'no' and so Holly was soon roaming free around the house, getting her bearings. After supper I let her out into the small back yard and watched her play with Sally while Mother and I washed the dishes.

'I heard Sally tell you about Mr Pepper,' Mother said. 'Mrs Handley tells me he was wounded and had to be sent home. He looks fit and healthy enough, but I think he has a limp. Every time I saw him today he was using a walking stick. Anyway, he's employed and he's now writing about the war effort for the paper, but I believe he hopes to be a novelist.'

I said nothing. I liked to listen to Mother talk. She enjoyed local gossip and it was a trait I'd developed in recent years, even though I never indulged in repeating it.

'Anyway, I plan to invite him round for supper on Saturday night. It pays to be neighbourly.'

'Why would you do that, Mother?' I asked. 'We don't really know anything about the man.'

'No, but I intend to find out more.'

I sighed. Mother loved meeting new people.

'When your father was alive I used to entertain all the time,' she said. 'I miss those days. When will this interminable war end?'

'Well, at least Henry is safe and well,' I said reminding her of the letter.

'Well, he was some months ago, anyway,' Mother said. 'Didn't you notice the date on the letter?'

I realised then that I hadn't. I extracted it from my pocket. Ninth of February 1862. It was four months ago and soon after Henry had enlisted. I felt a terrible sick dread in the pit of my stomach and prayed we would hear from him again soon.

The next morning I said nothing to Sylvia about what I'd seen, and I forgot to mention finding Holly until later in the day, but I dutifully gave her the bunch of keys and she hurried away to return them to Levy. If either she or Levy knew about the cat I'm sure they would mention her. At which time I would explain that I took her home because I didn't know who she belonged to. But neither Levy nor Sylvia mentioned Holly. Perhaps it was because they had completely forgotten about the creature. They both obviously had other things to think about. And, although I suspected they had gone off somewhere together the night before, I forced myself not to think about what I had witnessed.

I thought instead about our mysterious new neighbour. For all we knew, this story about being a wounded soldier was all just a lie. I had caught only the briefest glimpse of him, but he seemed the reporter type somehow. Not that I knew that much about journalists. He had been rather forward though, speaking to me as though he already knew me, and so I was determined to dislike him right away.

'Did you hear about the murder last night?' asked Sylvia as I came out onto the shop floor.

'*Oy-yoy-yoy*,' said Levy. 'That's all we need on the shop floor today. Gruesome stories to entertain our customers.'

'Sorry Mr Levy,' I said, but Sylvia just snorted.

'What customers?' she said. 'We haven't even opened yet.'

Then she proceeded to tell me all about the dead body that had been found in an alley nearby.

'*Oy gevalt*,' said Levy. 'I didn't hear about that.'

'The news story said that they had been half eaten – probably by an animal or something. The reporter said that the police had made enquiries at the zoo but no animals had been reported missing.'

'That's terrible …' I said.

'You ladies need to make sure you take care going home,' Levy said. 'In fact, I'll escort you both this evening.'

'Thank you, Gerald,' Sylvia said, and I pretended not to notice her lapse in formality by calling him by his first name or how they looked into each other's eyes. Instead I went to open the shutters. *The sooner the day begins, the better*, I thought.

'Are you missing anything?' I asked Sylvia later.

'What do you mean?'

'A cat. Well a kitten really. Have you lost one?'

'Me? No. I can't stand the things. I'm allergic. They make me sneeze.'

This made Holly's appearance even more mysterious.

Holly met me at the door as I entered the house that evening. It was Saturday and I could smell the food Mother was preparing for our guest.

'Kat, is that you?' she called from the kitchen.

'Yes, Mother.'

'Go and get changed. Our guest will be arriving in half an hour and I'd like you to entertain him while I'm cooking.'

I sighed. 'Yes, Mother.'

Holly followed me upstairs. When she meowed it sounded just like she was saying 'Hello'. It was a little strange how she appeared to be attempting to have a conversation with me. I wasn't used to cats; Mother had never let us have pets. But she didn't seem to mind Holly and I think this was because Sally really liked the animal. All in, she seemed to be a very intelligent creature.

In my room, Holly jumped up onto my bed and proceeded to groom her fur while I began to strip off my uniform.

Mother had put out an evening gown for me of red satin. I pulled my hair down out of the severe bun and brushed it vigorously. It was a relief to take out all of the pins. I dressed quickly and then remembered that this gown was a little low cut. I was about to change it for something else but became distracted when Holly stood up on the bed and began to meow in the most anxious fashion.

She jumped across to the dressing table and howled at the window.

'What is it, Holly?' I said. I pulled aside the curtain and glanced down into the street, but all I could see was an old man staggering along the sidewalk. The man didn't look very well. He was holding his arm against his chest as though he had injured it. Even so, he didn't appear to be in any immediate danger, so I dropped the curtain back down over the window.

Holly hissed at it. 'What's upset you so much? There's nothing there.'

The cat stared at me with her wide and pretty eyes. *If only I could understand you,* I thought. Then, shrugging, I fastened up my dress and hurried downstairs just in time to open the door to our guest, Mr George Pepper.

I couldn't help observing that Pepper was a rather handsome man. Though not especially tall, he had pale blue eyes and very blond hair. He was wearing a smart purple velvet smoking jacket, white shirt and an expensive cravat. The odd thing was he was carrying a cane, yet didn't appear to need it. I assumed he was one of those men who liked to carry them as a fashion accessory.

The cane was made of sturdy wood, with a handle that was carved to look like a lion's head, but actually on close inspection, the carving turned out to be a cat. I noticed as he sat down that he never actually put the cane down, but clung to it as though it afforded him some security.

'Ah, Mr Pepper,' said Mother, coming out of the kitchen. 'Dinner won't be long. Have you met my daughters, Katherine and Sally?'

Pepper was the height of propriety but I found him to be quite reserved despite his lapse when he spoke to me in the street. He had a sincere expression on his face when he bent to kiss my hand, and now properly introduced I led him into the parlour and poured sherry from the decanter into small glasses.

'Can I have some sherry?' asked Sally.

'Certainly not,' I said, holding out the glass to Mr Pepper. Sally pouted and sat down in the corner on Mother's chair. She was wearing a white taffeta dress and a bold red ribbon around her rag-roll curls.

'Thank you, Miss Lightfoot,' Pepper said.

'Kat,' I corrected.

'And who is this?' Pepper asked, smiling down at Holly. I had completely forgotten about the cat again and she had followed me into the parlour, hiding behind my skirt.

'This is Holly,' Sally explained, coming out of her sulk. 'Kat found her at Tiffany's.'

'You found her?' Pepper said.

'Yes. It was a little strange actually. She was in the safe, yet when I asked my co-workers none of them admitted losing her. I have no idea how she got in there.'

'Strange,' said Pepper. 'But cats are very mysterious creatures. They have their own logic and they can often be found in unexpected places. My grandfather once told me that a cat will chose its own home and a human to have as a pet.'

I laughed at this. 'Humans as the pets?'

Holly meowed. Pepper glanced at her and smiled.

'Good,' said Pepper. 'I'm pleased to see you have Holly. She has obviously chosen you for a reason. Cats are extremely useful to have around during these trying times.'

'*Whatever* are you talking about, Mr Pepper?'

'Please call me George,' he said. 'Have you been reading the newspapers? I suppose you've heard about the murder?'

I was just about to point out to Pepper that I didn't think this would be a suitable topic for Sally's ears when Mother came into the room.

'Your sherry, Mother.' I held out the glass and then excused myself to go and lay the table for her. When I returned, Pepper and Mother were getting along well and he was regaling her with humorous tales of his minor tour in the war effort. I was surprised that anything funny could be found about war. But Mother enjoyed his story about the cook who *couldn't* cook and the young soldier who lost his boot in the marshes and hobbled three miles before he noticed. The way Pepper told these stories it made the march seem like fun – that all of the soldiers found the experience to be a humorous adventure – but I thought I saw something in his expression that made me believe his tales were all invented.

'I believe you are going to write a book,' Mother commented. 'Will this be about your experiences in the war?'

Pepper's face darkened briefly. 'I don't think so. The novel is going to be fiction and I doubt that anyone would believe some of the things I saw in the South.'

'What did you see in the South?' asked Sally rudely.

'Things that would give you nightmares,' Pepper said, feigning sincerity for a moment and then his face lit up. 'But not to worry, you've got a lovely little cat there!'

Mother and I exchanged glances. Clearly Mr Pepper was much damaged in the war, but neither of us was going to probe the truth from him. I took Sally out of the room on the pretext of helping me with the table and then gave her a lecture that even Mother would have been proud to deliver.

'Stop badgering him. It's very rude,' I concluded.

Despite Pepper's light-hearted tales it was obvious to me that the war had been a most unpleasant experience for him. It was why we accepted his oddities. Such as randomly speaking to women he didn't know in the street. Or the unusual things he had said about cats. All the same, I found myself watching Holly closely that evening as she played with Sally. Something about her sudden appearance just didn't seem right and no-one at work was owning up to having her there. Could it be that she *chose* me as Pepper had suggested?

Five

The next day was Sunday. Tiffany's was closed and I was able to rest, reading the newspaper, while Mother and Sally went to church. Mother had long since stopped trying to force me to go with her, because it usually ended in arguments. I didn't believe in God or the supernatural and I didn't want to spend my only morning off on my knees in a cold, damp building listening to the hypocritical rants of Father Jack Ferrier. Everyone in the neighbourhood knew he was a drunk and a letch. Everyone except Mother, that is, who couldn't somehow see his faults at all.

I was still in my night robes, but the sound of something falling through the letter box penetrated the relaxed and lazy fugue I was in. I forced myself to get up to see what it was.

The letter sat in plain view on the mat and I recognised

one of the scented envelopes that Mother had given Henry for his mail. This one, however, was addressed to me. Sunday was of course a very unusual day for mail to arrive. Even so, I tore open the envelope and pulled the letter free. Henry's usually neat penmanship was harsh and untidy. It appeared to be rushed.

Kat,

Things have been a little strange around here. Yesterday we captured a band of deserters from the Confederate Army. They said they were heading north and that we should turn back if we knew what was good for us. They said that there was something evil in the trees.

Colonel Kendal laughed this off. 'It's some trick to make you all scared to go on, boys. Those crazy Southerners think us Yankees are afraid of our own shadows. But we'll show them, won't we? We're not afraid of anything.'

My comrades were rallied by the speech, but I'd been present when Kendal interviewed the leader of the deserters. He said that their own men were turning into monsters. That they were … Kat, I can't even bring myself to write of the horrors he spoke in this letter. I'd hate to leave such images in your mind.

The thing was, the man was totally sincere

about all of it. I don't believe he was lying. He was genuinely terrified.

Since then, despite everything the Colonel says, I've been scared too. I don't know why.

I had to tell someone about this and I'm so sorry to burden you with my irrational fears. I guess this war is getting to me. I hope you don't think me a coward.

Henry

PS Please don't show this to Mother. She will only worry.

I re-read the letter over and over again and then hid it in my reticule. I didn't think this would be such a good thing to show Mother, and even if Henry hadn't specifically asked me not to, I doubt I would have thought it wise. It was peculiar that he would write to me like this. He and I hadn't been close in years. Like all siblings we had had some differences, but I did love my brother and I felt a deep concern for him. I felt an intense anxiety at the thought of him marching towards the south, maybe wearing only one boot because he had lost the other in the marshes. I closed my eyes and tried to imagine Henry striding proudly across the country with his platoon, but I couldn't shake this hideous thought. Pepper's jokes were as sinister to me as the reality that Henry hinted at. Both of them hid something dark and ominous: a truth that was not being told.

There was hunger, malice and desperation in the watchful gaze of a thousand sets of glowing eyes that kept vigil from deep within the forest.

Union soldiers passed by, dragging their blistered feet through thick mud. The men were bedraggled, worn by battle and the constant march to find the enemy. No longer a proud troop of men believing God was on their side, the shambling horde was barely recognisable as human. They were almost dead on their feet: walking sleepers in the midst of their worst nightmare.

One of the men at the back of the line stopped. It was as though he knew his time had come and running was useless. The others were so wrapped up their own misery that they didn't notice him pause.

Bright eyes blinked as shadows poured from the forest and surrounded the soldier. There was no sound; even the night owls were silenced as he abandoned himself to the darkness, arms spread as though in some form of ritual sacrifice.

Henry turned then, and looked back at the twisted, hungry faces of his men. Then he looked beyond them, as though some sixth sense permeated his tired and befuddled mind. He saw the dark shapes fall on the lone man. Henry yelled.

His comrades turned to see what was happening. Some

stared with open mouths that screamed in silent horror, others began to run ahead, trying to put some distance between themselves and the bloodthirsty creatures behind them. But Henry began to fight his way back through the masses.

'Come on, Lightfoot,' gasped Colonel Kendal. He grabbed Henry's arm as the darkness turned towards them. 'It's not your time yet!'

'Kat,' said Henry. 'I'm scared of the darkness.'

My eyes flew open and I realised that I had drifted off in the chair. I felt a momentary nausea as the fear from the nightmare sank into my conscious brain. I was trembling and so rubbed the sleep away from my eyes and tried to steady my hands. Holly climbed on my knee and I stroked her soft fur until calm returned to me.

The newspaper I'd been reading fell to the floor at my feet. Holly meowed and jumped off my knee onto the paper and, as I wrestled it free from her playful paws, I noticed a bold headline: 'More Dead Found in Central Park'.

I picked up the paper. It was another animal attack.

Mother and Sally came into the parlour. 'Not up yet?' said Mother.

'I nodded off in the chair,' I explained.

'Poor you. I think you've just been working too hard.'

I was still shaken by my dream but pushed the thought of it away as I turned the page, looking for more information on the attacks, and found instead something equally strange. 'Theft From Morgue' read the headline, and the text:

> Yesterday a spokesman for the Mayor announced a recent rash of crimes in local hospitals. Bodies have been going missing from morgues and funeral homes all over the city.

'So, anything interesting happening?' Mother asked, sitting down beside me as she removed her gloves and Sally began to play with Holly.

I shook my head but didn't look up as I read the article.

'Well, you do seem rather engrossed ...'

'Sorry.'

Mother leaned over and looked down at the newspaper. 'Oh, dear. How dreadful!'

'Yes it is, isn't it?'

'Not that,' Mother said. 'The worst has happened. Hanging around with shop girls, you've suddenly turned into one of *those* people.'

I looked up from the paper. 'Whatever do you mean?'

'Someone who likes to read about other people's miseries.'

'Mother! I'm most certainly not like that!'

'Then why does this hold such morbid fascination for you?'

I couldn't answer. It was true that the stories of the dead bodies did fascinate me, and I really didn't know why. I had the most peculiar feelings about it. It was horrible to read, but somehow important too. The dream of Henry in the forest floated behind my eyes again. I shook my head, but the thought nagged at me that there was some kind of connection. I mean, why would anyone be stealing bodies from morgues? My mind flashed back to the previous evening. The man in the alley. A shudder ran up my spine and I thought of that awful saying that some people used when this happened … had someone just walked over *my* grave?

'I'm taking Holly into the yard,' Sally said and, as if the cat completely understood her, it followed the excited child out of the parlour.

There's something very peculiar about that cat, I thought.

I put aside the newspaper. 'I better go and get dressed,' I said. 'Perhaps we should all go out for a walk before lunch. It's such a nice day.'

'You go dear. You look as though you need the air. Take Sally with you,' suggested Mother. 'You know how tiresome she gets when she's bored.'

Six

'Let's stop running around like *meshugginas* – it's *only* a dead body! We have customers to serve.' Levy shouted over the chaos in the kitchen. A few of the workshop girls were yelling and crying in, mostly, over-dramatic, feigned shock.

'What's happened?' I asked, entering the room from the corridor. I had heard the commotion as I hung up my coat.

'A man attacked Edward and he had to shoot him,' Sylvia whispered. 'The police have taken the body away now. They think it was an attempted robbery on the store but Edward said ...'

Sylvia's voice dropped even lower and she took my arm, pulling me into the corridor and down towards the shop.

'Edward said that the man tried to *bite* him.'

'That's awful. Is Edward all right?'

'A little shook up I think, but mostly okay. He's a security guard, he's used to dealing with attempted break-ins,' Sylvia said.

I felt a strange certainty that I knew which man had attacked Edward. 'What did he look like?'

'I don't know. Ed said he was kind of, well dressed. He was lying amongst the trash cans and he thought the guy had been a victim of an attack or something. He went to help him and the guy went crazy.'

Levy came down the corridor behind us. 'I'm hoping you two are going to be sensible at least.'

'Of course, Mr Levy,' I said.

'Let's open up. The world has gone crazy. Just 'cos some *schmuck* tries to rob the store, he ends up dead, the girls are all screaming and hysterical. Women! *Oy-yoy-yoy*, this could ruin our sales for the day.'

Mr Levy wandered into the shop, wringing his hands and shaking his head. I smiled at Sylvia, shrugged, and then we followed him in. Levy was, despite himself, rather amusing sometimes.

Our first customer of the day was a little old lady and her grandson. 'I'm looking for a present for my daughter-in-law.'

I smiled at her and stayed behind the counter, giving her ample opportunity to look around. A few seconds later a young couple came in and began to browse the paste brooches. Then a soldier on leave came in. Before we knew it, the shop was full and Sylvia and I had trouble coping with the enquiries. We had to get Martin downstairs to help as well as Mr Levy.

As I wrapped a silver locket for the old lady, she bent over the counter and whispered, 'So tell me then … who did the guard kill?'

I stepped back, a little shocked, then rapidly finished the gift-wrapping and tied the small package with ribbon.

'I really couldn't talk about that, Madame,' I said, pursing my lips in the way I'd seen Sylvia do when she didn't want to be questioned.

The old lady took her package and left but she wasn't impressed that I refused to gossip.

The day continued in that manner. I went from customer to customer, only to be asked the same question.

'Bad news sure travels fast around here,' I said to Martin later. 'People are so strange about death. They all seem to really enjoy it.'

'It's human nature to be morbidly curious,' he answered. 'Want to see my latest remodelling of the handgun? I've done something remarkably clever. Even if I do say so myself!'

I followed Martin upstairs. It was the end of the day and all of the workshop girls had gone home. I thought about how Mother would disapprove of my being alone with Martin like this, but he was obviously harmless and very into showing off his latest inventions. I had become the person he confided in, because I showed interest, whereas Levy and Sylvia were interested only in each other. Despite my curiosity, I tried not to think about their relationship too much, but now that I was aware of it, the sultry looks and small exchanges between them were quite obvious.

In Martin's workroom everything was as usual with the exception of the gun. The Remington was lying on a table in the middle of the room and it seemed to have acquired a small metal tank, one foot long and six inches wide, that was attached to some brown leather straps. The tank linked to a new cylinder cartridge – a bulbous tube – and it had what looked like a clock key on it.

'In theory, you would wind up the key as far as possible and the clockwork mechanism I've installed is then activated. Then it runs the bullets through the box and the weapon can be fired automatically.'

'I understand the clockwork side, but what do you mean by "automatically"?' I asked.

'As your finger squeezes the trigger, the bullets keep firing until the mechanism needs rewinding, you stop squeezing, or you run out of bullets. Whichever comes first. Inside this cartridge there are over a hundred bullets.'

Martin opened the tank and I saw inside the most intricate mechanism.

'It's a large magazine,' I said.

'Yes! I knew you'd understand.'

The magazine held diamond off-cut bullets on what appeared to be a tiny conveyor belt that ran around into the metal box. He demonstrated how the magazine worked by manually moving the conveyor. As each bullet reached a certain point it was ejected by a small hammer that propelled it into a tube that led directly into the new, hollow cylinder cartridge.

I picked up the gun and the metal box, which was heavier than it looked.

'I couldn't make it any lighter,' Martin commented as I frowned, 'which is why it would be worn strapped to your back.'

'Martin, this is incredible. But why make it? Who would buy it?'

'It's a folly,' Martin shrugged. 'I like to challenge myself. But imagine our boys each having one of these on the battlefield? The war would be won and we would all be able to get our lives back to normal.'

I didn't approve of the war, because too many people had already died in the name of the cause. It seemed that many more would die at the hands of anyone wielding Martin's clockwork weapon, so I was torn between my love of his creativity and the horrible use to which it had been put.

'Of course, I have no idea if it would really work,' Martin said.

'You haven't tested it?'

'This is not really the right environment. I would

need an open field where there is no risk of anyone getting injured. But the mechanism definitely works, so theoretically the bullets should fire without any difficulty.'

One thing did occur to me and I said it to Martin. I wondered how quickly the magazine could be reloaded.

'I hadn't thought about that,' he said. 'Because, if you haven't killed the enemy with more than a hundred bullets, then the enemy can't be beaten … However it's a good thought and I must consider the problem. After all, the magazine is quite heavy, and how many spares could one soldier carry?'

I left him then and went downstairs in time to see Levy helping Sylvia on with her coat.

'We're getting a carriage home, would you like a lift?' Sylvia asked.

'No thanks, it's still bright and sunny out. I think the walk would be quite pleasant,' I said smiling.

I thought that Levy looked relieved that they didn't have to drop me home first. He and Sylvia were going somewhere alone again I guessed. But I was more relieved not to share a carriage with them. The tension in the air in close quarters was palpable.

'See you in the morning,' Sylvia said.

Walking home, my mind was full of Martin's inventions. He seemed obsessed with weapons for some reason and I wondered if this was because we were all so fixated on war these days. Some of Martin's gadgets were timesaving and wonderful. Like the dialight that he used to cut the diamonds. It made the cuts sharper and more accurate, apparently. There was also his tea-maker. Martin had discovered a way to boil a kettle by generating power from steam. He used a mini boiler fire in which he burned a piece of coal. This created steam that in turn ran a small engine, 'not unlike trains,' Martin had explained, and it warmed the water. The water then filtered slowly through the tea leaves that hung in a small muslin basket above a cup. I'd tasted the tea once and it was really good.

Martin was probably the smartest person I knew, and I was really enjoying watching his confidence grow as he showed me his creations. It was art to him. I guessed that jewellery design had become so easy that he needed something else to challenge his talents.

I passed by the gates of a small church. It had a green park within the grounds that was frequented by courting couples. I glanced in to see a young couple strolling arm in arm with their chaperone lagging behind them. The man was in uniform. He wasn't exactly handsome, but there was something so attractive about seeing a soldier wearing his uniform. He looked smart and heroic without really trying. The woman, well dressed in a formal day suit of brown and cream, was young and pretty with light brown hair.

The chaperone was a sour-faced old crone, unfortunately.

They always are, I thought, remembering when

Henry had walked out with Isabelle Formby. Her aunt had looked just like this woman. I suspected that she was some shrivelled old spinster too. Of course Isabelle had soon found herself a new beau when Henry enlisted, a banker twice her age, and I had heard tell that she would be marrying him in the autumn.

I walked on, musing about the weird turns and twists in life, when a terrible scream ripped through the air. It was coming from the park. I turned around, looking back at the couple, and saw the old woman throwing herself on the man in what appeared to be a fit of extreme rage.

She tore at his hair, while the girl screamed again. I didn't want to get involved, but I found myself hurrying back towards them. The soldier pushed the old woman back and away from himself. She fell over, and rolled on the grass.

'Aunt Mary?' wailed the girl. 'What's *wrong* with you?'

I reached them as Aunt Mary began to stagger to her feet. She looked both frail and strong, which was an oxymoron I know, and she appeared to be utterly insane.

Aunt Mary snarled like a rabid wolf. Her jaws snapped together and her neck cracked left and right like she had an annoying twitch that she couldn't control. Her eyes were bloodshot, the pupils almost filling her irises.

'It's the darkness,' said the soldier. His face was grey. 'It has even followed me home.'

The soldier took out his gun and pointed it at Aunt Mary. The old woman hobbled towards him with deliberate malice. My stomach turned at the sight of her twisted expression. Hate and greed. And yes, there was darkness in her. I could almost make out a black stain in the air around her. It was as though fog had sunk deep into her soul and it reminded me of the man in the alley behind Tiffany's.

'Come little soldier and play with me,' she said in a sing-song little girl voice. Then she began to hum a lullaby that I recognised but couldn't name. It was the most grotesque thing I had ever witnessed in my life.

The girl was sobbing uncontrollably now and I put my arm around her shoulders, as Aunt Mary dived once more at the soldier.

His gun fired. I saw, as though in a dream, the bullet enter her forehead, a red blossom-shaped pattern spread between her eyes as the shell exited the back of her head. Bits of brain, hair and skull exploded over the grass like a spray of red rain as Aunt Mary fell backwards.

My hand flew to my mouth as the woman landed on the ground with a sickening thump.

The girl slumped and I caught her, waving my hand before her face to try to stop her from fainting.

The soldier approached Aunt Mary and I saw that the old woman's body was still twitching. It was as though some demon possessed her and was still fighting to retain control.

My mind screamed at me to look away but I found I couldn't. And so, I watched the soldier pause over her, gun still pointed while Aunt Mary writhed and spat blood up at him. *Surely she couldn't still be alive?* The soldier stepped back, then aimed and fired again.

One, two, three, four, five … His gun was a Remington 1858. Thanks to Martin I could recognise the model and knew that the man had emptied his entire magazine into the old woman. Yet still he stood there firing empty rounds at the now still corpse.

The girl beside me choked on her sobs, giving way finally to the swoon that had tried to consume her. Not strong enough to hold her up, I lowered her down to the ground and placed my reticule under her head.

Several people came running, including a police officer who must have heard the gunfire.

'What's happened here?' asked the officer.

I didn't know what to say, because I hadn't understood the incident at all.

'It's all right, officer,' said a voice I recognised. 'This soldier was just doing his duty.'

At that moment, George Pepper pushed his way through the crowd and approached the soldier. 'She's dead,' he whispered, and then he prized the gun from the man's fingers and led him away to talk privately with the officer.

All of this unfolded in front of me as though I had stepped into a strange and illusory world. I felt a fog of shock drowning out my senses. The chattering of the people around me receded. Even the birds had stopped singing in the trees. But one thing stood out to me, despite my astonishment at what had happened: I couldn't help noticing how Mr Pepper clung to his cane and continued to look nervously at the trees that lined the path. I turned my head to glance at the foliage also, but could see nothing but the dull shadows I would have expected to find there.

Seven

'Kat! Where have you been? I've been so worried,' Mother said as I finally arrived home.

'I'll explain everything,' Pepper said, walking in behind me. 'Kat has had a nasty shock. It's certainly something that a young lady should not have had to endure.'

Mother went visibly pale at his words. 'What shock? What's happened?'

I wanted to hear Pepper's explanation, but Mother sent me up to my room to lie down. I was still very confused by what I had seen and I hoped that Pepper had made more sense of it than I had. Did I or did I not see something hovering around the old woman, for example? And why was Pepper so afraid of the trees?

I found Holly sleeping on my bed. I bent to stroke her and she raised her head and studied me carefully, licked my hand, then settled down and went straight back to sleep. I slipped off my walking boots and lay down beside the cat. I felt comforted by her presence for some reason. After the madness of the day, the normality at home was welcome. I felt shaken by the events, and more than a little scared. The soldier's words kept running through my head. *'It's the darkness'*, he had said, and it had struck a chord with me because of Henry's letter.

'Kat?' Mother called from downstairs. 'Mr Pepper has gone now. Come down please.'

I went into the parlour to find Mother pouring my tea and adding sugar even though she knew I didn't take it. 'For shock,' she said when she saw my expression.

'Mother, I'm perfectly fine.'

'I doubt that. You saw one of our brave soldiers losing his mind and killing an innocent woman. I'm sure that was horrifying, and I'm so sorry you had to witness it.'

'Is that what Mr Pepper told you?' I asked.

'Well, he said something about the woman being *possessed*, but I'm sure it had to have been the man. She was probably just protecting her charge.'

I shook my head. 'No, mother … the woman was …'

'Drink your tea before it gets cold, dear. It doesn't matter now. It's all finished and you should just try to forget the whole terrible incident.'

I sipped my tea, grimacing at the sickly-sweet taste. Mother always thought that tea was the cure for all that ails us. It was a representation of her attitude towards civilised behaviour. We mustn't discuss awful things. If it bothers us we drink tea until we forget. I had learnt that day that our society wasn't always civilised. And I had suspected for some time that this endless war was just another sign of our social decay. It had always been insane to me that we were fighting against our own countrymen.

I put the cup down. It was hard to be civilised right then. My mind kept flashing back to the demented old crone, and her face before and after the bullet destroyed her mind. The sight was haunting me. Where was civility in those glaring, rage-filled eyes? Where was any humanity? The woman had been out of her mind, I was sure of it, but there was no point in arguing the point with Mother, because it wouldn't have fit in with her view of the world.

I picked at the light supper she brought me, moving the food sufficiently around the plate to make her believe that I had eaten more than I had, because I really wasn't hungry. Then I excused myself and went to bed early. I thought that I wanted to be alone with my thoughts, and sleep was probably the best cure for the anxiety that was intermittently making my heart pound whenever the day's events flashed through my mind.

In my room I searched my reticule for Henry's letter. Once it was in my hands I studied the note, only to find that it contained no reference at all to 'the darkness' as my memory told me it had. No. I was mistaken. But where had I heard that expression before? I closed my eyes and then the awful dream I had came back to me. The horrible vision was inspired by Henry's letter. In my dream I had *seen* the darkness. This was why the old woman, and the soldier's behaviour, had not been as shocking as it should have been.

This is insane, I told myself. *My imagination has always been wild. There is no darkness. The soldier was damaged from his time in the war. My mind made the rest up.* But to believe this meant that my own sanity was at question, and I couldn't accept that I was the one who was insane. *No,* I thought again; this time with more certainty. I had seen and heard exactly what I thought I had. There was no question. But, for the sake of everyone else, I would pretend that I hadn't and hope that in time the horrors of that day would disappear from my thoughts.

I climbed into bed. Holly shifted as though she knew I needed more space. I had never let her sleep in my room before, but that night she gave me comfort.

I glanced at the oil lamp beside my bed. Mother was always talking about having gaslight fitted in the house, but we had been unable to afford it. I turned the lamp down but left a dull flame there as I really didn't want to sleep in the dark.

The next day, Mother received another letter from Henry. It was cheerful and happy, unlike the grim note I had received, and he talked about the forthcoming respite that he and the men hoped to have.

'Isn't that wonderful,' Mother said, bustling into the room. 'Henry's coming home soon! Kat, why are you dressed? Surely you don't mean to go into work today after the terrible shock you had yesterday?'

'Of course I must, Mother,' I said.

We argued about it briefly but I couldn't help noticing that Mother was rather proud of my resolve, despite her instinct to keep me home and safe that day. I couldn't forget what had happened but my sleep had been surprisingly restful with Holly's gentle purring to lull me. Going to work, taking my mind off everything, especially this new letter from Henry, seemed like the best cure. You see, I deliberately didn't ask the date of Henry's letter. I was afraid to.

Mother left my room saying she was going to call next door to see Mrs Handley, because the old lady hadn't been feeling too well. 'Will you make sure Sally eats breakfast before you leave? I'll probably be about half an hour.'

I finished getting ready and managed to pin Sally down for a few moments to eat some eggs with fresh bread and butter. After which she ran off to the yard to play. Then, as I was placing my lunch in my reticule, I heard Sally yelling.

I hurried through the kitchen and threw open the back door only to find a man, wearing the tattered remains of a Confederate uniform, standing between the gate to our yard and the alley behind.

'You gotta help me!' he said. 'The darkness is coming …
I can feel it in my blood.'

'Sally. Get inside! Now!' I said, and she edged away
from the wall where she cowered in fright. 'Please leave
our yard or I will be forced to send for the police. It won't
be good for you to be found here.'

I tried to keep my voice steady, but the man was
frightful to behold. He looked as though he had crawled
out of a pit of thick mud. I wasn't surprised that Sally had
been so frightened.

'Who is he?' she gasped, throwing herself into my
arms.

'I don't know,' I said.

'I'm so hungry …' the man said.

'Feed him. Then he'll go away,' Sally said, and I
marvelled at her logic, but I was afraid to encourage him
further into the yard.

It was unfortunate that the back gate had been left
unlocked. I knew Sally sometimes sneaked out the back
to her friend's yard a few doors down when Mother said
she couldn't go out.

'We're going inside,' I said. 'Please leave our yard.'

At that moment, Holly ran through the house to the
back door. She pushed her way round my legs and put
herself between the man and Sally and me. The cat hissed
and spat in a way I had never seen her behave before. She
was indeed a most mild-natured animal as a rule. The
soldier stared at the cat, then backed away from the yard.

'It's not my fault … It took me one night … I couldn't help it. I'm *so* hungry.' The soldier shuffled away and Holly followed him to the gate and seemed to watch him stagger away down the alley.

When the coast was clear, the cat looked back at me as if to say … *come on then, lock the gate.* I moved forward and secured the catch, then I took Sally back inside and waited for Mother to return before I left for work. I didn't tell her about the incident, but I made Sally swear never to leave the gate unbolted and not to sneak away anymore. Times were becoming very dangerous in New York City and it wasn't because of the threat that the war may come to us. It was because I feared that some related *thing* … some *darkness* had travelled here instead.

Tremors took me as I left the house. I felt as though I was always trying to keep my composure for everyone else's sake. As I reached the corner of our street I decided to hail a cab. For some reason I just didn't feel safe walking to Fifth Avenue. And so I climbed into the Hansom of the friendly and polite cabbie that always nodded to me on the way to work.

No-one seemed to notice that I had arrived at work later than usual, and the day started in the normal way. It was all a little too normal though, after all the excitement of the last few days. I was relieved to hear that Edward *hadn't* had to fend off any further burglars and that no *other* bodies had appeared in alleys nearby, but I found that one of the workshop girls, Agnes, was reading an article about the park incident the day before.

'Look at this, Kat,' Agnes said as I stowed my coat and reticule. 'Soldier on leave killed his chaperone. Obviously he didn't like her tagging along when he was walking out with his girl.'

'That's not very nice,' said Lizzie, entering the room in a hurry because she was clearly late again and didn't want Levy to notice. 'Besides, that's nothing. You should have seen the fight that broke out in the corridor of our boarding house. This bloke came in and started talking about how dark it was. It was really silly considering they have gaslight and it was on full.'

'What happened?' asked Agnes.

Lizzie went quiet for a minute. 'It was a bit … grisly to be honest, Agnes. I'm not sure …' then Lizzie looked at me as though she expected me to faint at the idea.

'Go on,' I said.

'Well. The neighbour's husband, Francis, came back worse for wear as usual. Then this other guy, he only moved in a few weeks ago, came out and started to yell at Francis to be quiet. Francis likes to sing when he's full of beer … and it can be very annoying at two in the morning. Anyway, they started to have this row and Francis got all upset, said he couldn't see. That it was *dark*, or something like that. My sister, Pauline, says the cheap hooch was probably turning him blind.

'Anyway, things started to get out of hand. The guys

started to fight and then Francis *bit* the new guy. Actually took a chunk out of him! The guy yelped. Then he hit him, and Francis fell down the stairs.

'When his wife, Agatha, came out to get him, there was blood all over the bottom step, but Francis was nowhere to be seen. Agatha went outside in her nightgown, but Pauline and I persuaded her to come back in. No use being out alone like that in that part of town.'

'That's terrible,' I said.

'Yeah,' nodded Lizzie. 'But that's not the worst of it. The new guy started wailing at six this morning. The landlord knocked on his door, and when he got no answer he used his spare key to get in. He found his tenant in a terrible state and had to send for a doctor.'

'What was wrong with him?' I asked.

'The bite became infected. His arm was all swollen up and he was feeling really sick. Pauline said he might have to have it amputated.'

'Urgh!' said Agnes.

At that moment, Levy came into the room and shooed Agnes and Lizzie up to the workroom. 'What're you sitting around here for like a load of *shleppers*. Work already!'

I went out into the shop to find that Sylvia had already opened the shutters. There were no customers in but she was looking out into the street as though expecting someone.

'What's wrong?' I asked.

'Nothin', she said, turning away from the window. I glanced out in the general direction she had been looking and could see the street was still quite empty. Then our first customer of the day entered.

Half an hour later, the initial rush hit a lull and the shop was briefly empty. Sylvia and I took this opportunity to change some of the trays in the window.

'We'll put in those new sets of eternity rings,' I suggested.

'I'll go and get them from the stockroom,' Sylvia said. 'I'll need to open the cupboard, Mr Levy.'

Levy followed her, while unclipping a bunch of keys from around his belt. I opened the doors that covered the window display. As I bent forward to retrieve the first tray that we needed to replace, I found myself face to face through the glass with an old man.

He had longish white hair and pale, watery blue eyes. His clothes were clean but threadbare and he was staring intently at the wedding band display. He looked up and nodded to me. I thought he had very sad eyes and I smiled at him and nodded back. Then he turned and walked away quickly.

At that moment, Sylvia and Levy returned with the new display trays and we began to change them over.

That afternoon I saw the old man again. This time he was across the street. He was watching the shop and I felt strangely uncomfortable at the thought. Why was he hanging around out there? What was he actually looking at? After that, whenever I was near the window, I noticed the man was still there. I was about to comment on it to Sylvia when Levy called out from the stockroom and she went in there to help him with something. Then some more customers came in and we became so busy that I forgot about him.

Eight

'Well would you look at that?' I said to Sylvia a few days later. 'That man is there again.'

Sylvia's cheeks flushed as she looked out into the street. It was six o'clock and the store had just closed for the day. 'I don't see anyone,' she said anxiously.

The man had disappeared.

'It's this old guy. He's always hanging around outside like he's waiting for someone. He seems harmless enough, but he looks a little sad to me.'

'What did he look like?' Levy asked.

'White hair, about 60, I think,' I said. 'I only got a quick look at him close up.'

'*Close up?*' Sylvia said, her voice pitched higher than usual.

'Yeah. He was looking in the window when we changed the display.'

ZOMBIES AT TIFFANY'S

'I didn't see anyone looking in the window,' Sylvia said. 'Are you sure you weren't imagining it?'

My back prickled. I was offended by the idea that Sylvia might think I would imagine things. 'Certainly not. It was when you and Mr Levy were fetching the stock and I was alone. I think he hadn't been expecting me to open the cases and look out at him.'

'What was he looking at?' Levy asked.

'Wedding rings …'

Sylvia left the shop floor and hurried away into the back.

'What's up with her?' Levy asked.

I shrugged. 'I don't know, Mr Levy. I'll go and check on her.'

I followed Sylvia into the kitchen and saw her pulling her coat on. 'Will you tell Mr Levy I had to go? I'm not feeling so good.'

'Sylvia, if you're sick don't you think you should wait? I'm sure Mr Levy will give you a ride home.'

'What do you mean?' Sylvia snapped.

'I just thought …'

'Well don't think. There's nothing going on between Mr Levy and me. He's kind to me. That's all. He's a married man, you know.'

'Sylvia, I didn't mean …'

'Please. Just tell him I had to leave.'

Sylvia hurried out and I returned to the shop floor to help finish the daily clean-up. Levy looked confused when I told him that Sylvia had left.

'Right. That's enough for today. I'm going to lock up and leave as well. Do you need a ride home?' he asked.

I felt uncomfortable about accepting the ride without Sylvia there, so I politely declined. Levy wasn't offended. Again he looked relieved, so I was glad I hadn't put him out. He probably wanted to get home to his family.

'Good. I'll see you tomorrow then,' Levy said before hurrying away. I couldn't help comparing his exit with Sylvia's.

It was raining when I eventually left the building, and I was beginning to regret not taking Levy up on his offer of a lift home. I pulled on my gloves, secured my hat firmly on my head and raised the collar of my jacket up as I stepped outside.

'Can you help me?'

The old man's voice was old and weak, and his presence outside the trade entrance gave me a shock. Even though he looked unthreatening, the suddenness of his arrival made me feel nervous. Especially after the events that had unfolded over the last few days. You never could tell these days, with all of the crazy things that were happening in the city. I glanced back at the closed door and considered calling for Edward.

'Miss, I'm not here to hurt you,' the man said. 'I just need your help in getting to talk to my wife.'

Although I had never been anywhere outside of

Manhattan, I knew that this man wasn't from around here. He had a Southern drawl and it reminded me of the Confederate soldier who had invaded our yard and scared Sally so much.

'I'm sure I don't know your wife, sir,' I answered politely. 'Is she one of our regular customers?'

The man shook his head sadly. 'Susan is my wife. She works here.'

I glanced at the door again. I really wasn't happy with how this was going. I knew all of the girls working at Tiffany's and I was certain that there wasn't a Susan among them. I ran through all of the workshop girls' names in my head. *Agnes, Lizzie, Maude, Emily, June, Hermione.*

'I'm sorry, that name is unfamiliar to me. I think you must be mistaken.'

'Why are you lying to me?' he asked sadly. 'I know she works with you. I seen her every day in the shop. You and she talk together sometimes.'

'You see, you are mistaken. That's not Susan, that's Sylvia,' I said.

'*Sylvia*? I never thought I'd see the day …'

The old man looked as though someone had hit him hard.

'Look. I'm sorry,' I said, 'but there must be some mistake. Maybe Sylvia resembles your wife? You see I know she isn't married. She doesn't wear a ring and …'

The man looked down at his hands. 'I could never

afford no fancy ring …'

'I have to go. Sorry. But its pouring with rain and I need to find a cab and get home.'

'Sure. Sorry to hold you up, Miss.' The old man turned and began to walk away.

I saw the sadness in his stooped shoulders as he left and I just couldn't help it. I had to run after him.

'Wait! You shouldn't be out on the streets on a night like this. Can I share my cab with you? Drop you home?'

'That's mighty kind of you, Miss …?'

'Lightfoot,' I said.

'My name's Judd Butler, Miss Lightfoot, and I'm right glad to meet you.' He shook my outstretched hand. 'Susie has a kind heart like you do. Look,' he said, holding out his pocket watch. He opened it and showed me the miniature painting of his wife. 'She's just so beautiful. She was 15 when we married ten years ago.'

I looked down at the portrait and there was no doubt in my mind that it was of Sylvia. The likeness was too close. I didn't know what to say for a moment.

'H-how did you meet?' I asked.

'Her Pa and me was friends. I fell in love with Susie from the first moment I saw her. It was only right that she should marry me when she was old enough.'

I felt a little sickened by this revelation. Sylvia liked older men. Her relationship – whatever that might be – with Levy proved that. But close up, Judd Butler looked too old to have been her husband. Even ten years ago when

Sylvia would have just been a child, Judd must have been nearly 50.

'Will you help me?' he asked. 'All I want is to git to talk with her. Find out why she run away.'

I hailed a cab to give me thinking time and waited while Butler gave his address. It was a boarding house a block past where I lived, but I decided it was best to take him home first. I wasn't sure I wanted him to know my address.

'The thing is, it's not my place to get involved,' I said as the cabbie cracked his whip and the horses began to trot down the street. 'I don't think Sylvia would thank me for that. She likes her privacy.'

'Please, Miss Lightfoot. I know Susie won't be mad at you. All you have to do is git her to a place where we can meet in private.'

The carriage pulled up outside of the hostel. I said goodbye to him without making any promises. 'I'll think about it, but I'm not sure what I can do.'

Butler stepped out of the cab and went towards the doorway. I watched him enter the hostel, then I pulled the door closed and signalled for the cabbie to move on.

The driver cracked his whip and the horses began to move forward. Then he turned the carriage around and headed back towards my address.

I slipped back into my thoughts, particularly pondering the revelation that Sylvia was married, and to someone like Judd. I wanted to help him, but knew I just shouldn't get involved.

At that moment the driver hauled back on the reins and the horses came to an abrupt halt. I almost fell off the seat but managed to catch hold of the leather strap above the door.

'What in tarnation …' shouted the driver.

I heard him dismount and then the sound of voices raised in argument. I slid down the window and looked out. I could see that another cab was lying half way across the wrong side of the street.

The other driver was shaking his head and protesting: 'I'm telling you, someone ran right out in front of me. I had to swerve to miss hitting him.'

'Where is he now then?' demanded my driver.

At that moment I heard something bang against the door on the opposite side of my carriage. I jumped and spun around to see the grinning, horrible face of a man that had been starved of all of his humanity. He glared in at me balefully with wide, shining, black eyes that glowed like embers in a fire. Then he began to bang on the door as though he had the right to be let in.

I think I squealed, but my heart was in my mouth and I was too frightened to scream. Instead I cowered back against the other door.

'Hey buddy! What's wrong with you? Get the fuck away from my customer.'

The man's hair was wild and unkempt, and as he turned his head, wet splashes hit the window. The water left pink streaks down the glass. He grinned as my driver approached him.

'Hey, that's him! He's the guy that ran in front of me!' called the other driver, and he came running at the man.

'What's wrong with you? You crazy or somethin'?'

The answer of course was *yes*. The man was insane. I knew it but couldn't say it, and I felt that there was evil around him. *In* him. It was like a cloak of darkness that surrounded him somehow. It was the same darkness that had haunted my dreams, and, I was certain, that I had seen around the chaperone in the park.

What happened next shocked me.. The wild man dived on the second driver, grabbing him by his thick coat. He pulled him off his feet with super-human strength and bit directly into his face. The driver screamed, blood spurted out from the wound, and as the lunatic pulled back, he also took a chunk of skin with him. The madman then glanced through the window and smiled at me, his teeth red and bloody.

As I watched, he began to chew the skin he had bitten off, as though it were a tasty morsel of meat he had been served in a fine restaurant.

Nausea overtook me and bile rose in my mouth. I tried to hold it back but it wouldn't stay. I turned, leaning over to the open window on my side of the carriage, and vomited out onto the pavement. Then I collapsed back into my seat, shaking while I removed my handkerchief from my pocket and wiped my mouth, tasting bile and sick on my tongue. By this time the two drivers had hold of the man and, because of the commotion, someone had alerted the police, who came running. After the recent events, they were on every street corner.

They threw the struggling madman into a prison carriage and took him away a short time later.

I stood in the rain as the police cart drove away. His arms were outstretched to me through the bars on the door at the back and he was still grinning. I was sickened to the core.

'I'm hungry …' he cried.

His voice carried through the rain and we stood in silence watching him go. A dense chill descended, like a thick miasma.

'Miss?'

I looked up to find my driver standing beside me.

'I'll take you home now. No charge. I'm so sorry you had to see this.'

'What on Earth is going on?' I asked.

'I don't know,' said the driver. 'But it sure ain't pretty.'

Holly greeted me cheerfully as I entered the house, rubbing up and around my feet. I decided against telling Mother what had happened. If she heard any more strange stories then I doubted she would let me out of her sight again, and I had to return to work. We needed the money!

Even so, she noticed that I was off my food that night.

ZOMBIES AT TIFFANY'S

It was hard to hide the fact that the liver and onions reminded me too much of the gore I had witnessed earlier that evening.

'Perhaps you're coming down with something?' Mother suggested.

'I'm just not hungry …' and saying those words made me feel somewhat better. 'Any news from Henry?'

Mother shook her head. 'No. But Mrs Handley's son, James, came home yesterday on leave.'

I listened as Mother told me all about James. He was a hero, but then everyone involved in the war effort was a hero to Mother.

'He's coming round for tea with Mrs Handley tomorrow,' Sally chipped in, 'and we're going to hear all about the war then!'

'Would you really want to hear any of that?' I asked Sally.

'Of course I would. It's so exciting.'

'Don't neglect your needlepoint, dear,' Mother said, and Sally reluctantly picked up the embroidery she had been working on.

The normality of our family unnerved me. It felt as though our home was a cocoon from the real world. Outside there was chaos, or so it felt that night, and Mother was blissfully unaware of it all. At Tiffany's there was that same sense too. Inside the shop, we were protected from the horrors of the streets. Perhaps New York had always been this dangerous, and I had previously been totally oblivious to it. If so, then I craved a return to those days of innocence. '

Lying in bed that night, sleep wouldn't come. I saw again the darkness in the wild-haired man and I thought I knew what it was. I wasn't religious by nature, preferring to leave that to Mother, but the idea of some inherent evil taking over men's souls wouldn't leave me. What I'd seen in that man's eyes – my imagination showed them glowing as though lit from within by red flames – had led me to believe that something bad was happening in our independent and modern city. Something I believed that could destroy us all.

I had to toughen up, mentally and physically, and arm myself, if we were to survive this and come through the other side unscathed.

Nine

On my way into work the next morning I saw the street urchin again. It had become a habit to share my lunch with the boy, but that morning I noticed something was wrong. He was staggering towards me and he looked hungrier than ever. Instinct, or maybe it was the strange things I had seen recently that had made me so wary, whatever it was, I felt an overwhelming urge to stay away from the boy and so I crossed the road and walked on the other side. The boy didn't seem to notice as he carried on walking down the street.

As I turned the next corner I glanced at my pocket watch to check the time. I felt a vague uneasiness that took form as a sick anxiety in the pit of my stomach. Mr Berry's milk cart was nowhere to be seen. The farmer was *never* late with his milk round.

On the next street I passed the row of cabbies. The

one that always doffed his hat to me sat on top on his carriage with his hat pulled down over his eyes. It was a warm morning, but he pulled his coat around him and sat as though the cold of winter had penetrated his bones. I noticed he had a thick bandage around one hand.

I hurried on towards Fifth Avenue, past the local church, and felt a little cheered when I saw a wedding party stepping down from their carriages in preparation for an early service. The wedding party made their way into the church grounds. They were lively and cheerful and at the time I didn't think about the day the chaperone had gone mad, or any of the other anomalies that were affecting the city.

The day is not all doom and gloom, thank goodness, I thought. And so I was able to push away the sick feeling, and even loitered long enough to see the bride arrive in her full glory, wearing an ivory dress of pure silk, decorated with hundreds of pearls. Despite the ostentation of the dress, she wore a simple wreath of flowers in her coiffured brown hair.

Tiffany's clientele was a mix of wealthy and poor. The shop tried to cater to all needs, which was why it had been so successful for so long. Sometimes it attracted people with money, but not always from the upper classes, and one such person came to the store that day. His name was Rocky Spinetti, and he was what Levy referred to as an *entrepreneur*: which meant, from what I could gather, that he was something of a businessman who took risks. Rocky was short, slightly overweight, and with the meanest face I had ever seen. He looked perpetually unhappy, as though he expected everyone in the shop to be rude to him. This would never happen at Tiffany's as the reputation was paramount. If Mr Levy ever caught any of us being rude or disrespectful to customers, then we would no longer be welcome to work there.

'Levy,' said Rocky. 'I want you to show Marlene some beautiful things. I ain't worried about the cost just as long as the lady is happy. Is that clear?'

I didn't like Rocky's attitude but I pretended not to notice how ill-mannered he was. I focused my attention instead on his girlfriend, Marlene. She was an attractive blonde and she wore finery of the sort that Lady Elsie might own. Unlike Lady Elsie, however, Marlene had little sense of style, and she mixed her clothing and jewellery in a way that showed a complete lack of taste. There was a twinkle in her eye that attracted me to her though. She seemed to be more alert than most people. It was as though she was always watching what everyone else was doing and responding to it in a way that was appropriate, but not necessarily natural.

'I want a ring, Rocky. You promised me a ring,' Marlene said. She had the kind of low-class, nasal accent that would set Mother's teeth on edge, but one thing working at Tiffany's had taught me was that you had to treat everyone the same. Despite Rocky's brash comment that he could afford anything in the shop, I led Marlene to a tray of rings that were lovely, but not too expensive. I didn't want to embarrass the man when he discovered that he really couldn't afford the best ones.

Marlene cooed over the rings. 'Oh, look at this one, Rocky …' she said as she tried them on, but Rocky showed little or no interest in any of them. Instead he wandered around the shop floor looking at the most expensive necklaces and diamond bracelets we had, and he showed a particular fascination with the area around the till.

'I wanna try that one!' said Marlene, and I put away the rings she had been admiring and retrieved the next tray. These were more expensive, but not by much.

'Hey, Marlene, what about this one?' Rocky said.

I looked up to see that Rocky was at the solitaire display. The rings there could cost hundreds of dollars each. Marlene left me and scurried over to the other counter. Sylvia was already over there waiting to help them, so I turned to see that Levy was watching Rocky closely. His mouth was pursed in a way that told me he was not at all happy. He nodded to Sylvia.

'I'm afraid I can't open this case today, Sir,' Sylvia said. 'The key was damaged and we're waiting for the locksmith to make a replacement.'

I knew this was a lie, so I raised my eyebrow at Levy.

'*Gonif*,' he whispered.

I noticed that Rocky half turned in our direction as though he had heard Levy utter the word. The man frowned but said nothing. Another customer came in and I served them while half-watching Rocky and Marlene move around the shop. Any minute I was convinced that Rocky was going to do something, but just as my customer left with a nice pair of cufflinks, another man appeared at the doorway.

The new man opened the door and glanced around without coming all the way in. He was well over six feet tall, stocky and was wearing a tight-fitting suit and tie.

'Mr Spinetti? You should see this?' he called.

Rocky and Marlene turned around. 'I'm busy,' said Rocky.

The big man seemed devastated, and he looked back over his shoulder at the street outside. He stepped into the shop and closed the door behind him, but remained there looking out into the street. After a moment, he turned back to his boss once more.

'Mr Spinetti. This is *urgent!*' he said.

Rocky turned and stared at him. The men's eyes locked, and after a moment, Rocky frowned and moved over to the door.

'What is it, Danny?'

I found myself coming round from behind the counter to stand beside Rocky.

Outside, a group of people were gathering on the other side of the street. It took me a minute of looking over this strange crowd as they hunched and shambled forward towards the door before I realised that something was wrong with them. They looked peculiar. At the front of the row was a woman in a wedding dress. Flowers were hanging from hair that had fallen out of a coiffure. Her ivory dress was decorated with hundreds of small white pearls. It was also smeared with brownish stains.

'No!' I gasped.

I recognised her as the bride I had seen emerge from her white carriage and walk serenely into the church earlier that day. But her shiny brown curls were now stained and wet looking. Beside her, the groom, I assumed, was wearing a torn tail-coat. His cravat was sliding loosely down the front of his dress shirt and there was a huge rip in his trousers. Around them was a collection of what appeared to be wedding guests in various states of disarray, including a small page boy and a flower girl who was still holding a basket of petals in her blood-stained fingers.

'The darkness,' I said. 'My God. It's finally here.'

'What are you talking about girl?' Rocky said sharply, but I could tell by the edge in his voice he knew already what was waiting outside.

'Close the shutters. Lock the doors,' I said urgently. '*Please* Mr Levy.'

Levy hurried over to the door. 'What is this?' he said.

'What's wrong with their eyes?' Sylvia asked, coming up behind me.

'I've seen this before. Last night when I took a cab home … Also the other day in the park, and then there was the Confederate soldier in our back yard …'

'I think you ought to go in the back for a break, Miss Lightfoot,' Levy said, giving me a strange look. 'I don't think you are feeling too well.'

'I'm feeling perfectly fine thank you,' I said. 'Now get these goddamn shutters down.'

'Now, wait a minute …' said Levy.

'You heard the lady,' Rocky interrupted. 'Danny, get out there and close those shutters.'

Danny sprang into action, as did Rocky with a degree of agility that didn't seem possible given his size and shape. I hurried out behind them, snatching the keys from Levy's belt as I did so. Sylvia and Levy stared at us. I realised that this was the first time I had seen them with nothing to say.

As Danny reached the first shutter and pulled it down, I locked it and glanced worriedly over my shoulder. The horde of people twitched in unison.

'I'm hungry …' said the bride.

'It's dark …' said the groom.

'What's going on? You got some *chutzpah* taking my keys like that …' Levy said, emerging to try to wrestle the keys from my hands.

'You see these people?' I said. 'They are dead. All of them. And they are hungry. Do you know what that means?'

'You're crazy!'

'No she ain't,' Rocky said. 'I seen this before too. We

gotta get inside.'

Levy turned around and faced the group of people. They were now shuffling forward, coming towards the shop. 'You people,' he shouted. 'Clear the street or I'm going to send for the cops.'

I locked the final shutter then returned to the door with Rocky and Danny. 'Mr Levy, please come inside.'

The horde was grinning. Hungry mouths and empty souls needed to be fed, and they were picking up speed. I wasn't at all sure that locking the shutters could hold them off, but I hoped it would at least delay them from getting inside.

'I'm warning you,' said Levy. 'Stop this creepy shit right now or I'm *machen a gevalt!*'

At that moment the bride sprang away from the group and ran straight towards Levy. It sparked a reaction in the others, and the wedding party from hell began to run across the street in rapid pursuit.

Danny grabbed Levy, dragging him inside. He pulled the door grille closed just as the bride reached it. I ran the bolt, then turned the key in the locks. The bride's hands reached through the large gaps in the grille and Danny slapped them back, before he drew a gun from his inside pocket and shot her square in the face.

The bride fell back into the waiting arms of the groom. He grinned at us, blood and saliva dripping down over his chin as he bent down and bit into her dead scalp. The others fell on the body and I let myself be propelled backwards into the shop as Danny slammed the main door closed.

'Oh my God. Omigod …' Sylvia said. She was as pale as a ghost and shaking from head to foot as I pulled the interior blind down over the door to cut out the sight of the dead horde eating their former companion.

'What are they?' Levy said. His eyes were wide with shock. 'What the fuck are they?'

We waited, expecting a barrage against the door at any minute. I could hear the sickening sounds of bones breaking and flesh tearing, and my vivid imagination filled in the blanks. I was certain that the monsters were ripping the bride apart.

It went quiet again very soon and then I heard sobbing outside the door.

'Killed her … gone and killed her. My Cecilia. But … was hungry … so hungry and cold and the darkness keeps surrounding me …'

I met Rocky's eyes and I knew that he had told the truth when he said he had seen this before. Perhaps he even understood it better than I did. I glanced at him and Danny. They were alert, and for the first time I saw that Rocky was also carrying a gun. Marlene was seated in a corner on one of the chairs we had placed around the shop for customers. She was gazing at her nails but making no fuss at all, much to my surprise. She had originally struck me as someone who would. It was as though she was used to unusual things happening around her.

'Perhaps I ought to go and speak to Edward?' I said.

Mr Levy fingered the Star of David he had on a chain around his neck. His lips were moving, and I guessed he was praying.

'Mr Levy?' I said again.

Levy looked up at me and I could see his eyes were a little distant. He blinked, and returned to us in the shop. 'Yes. Good idea. Perhaps we can send Edward out to get the police?'

'We're not sending Edward out to face … them,' I said firmly.

Levy glared at me but didn't disagree.

'Sylvia, perhaps you could make us all some tea?' I suggested. 'I'm going to speak to Martin and the workshop girls. They need to know what's going on out there.'

I left Sylvia in the kitchen and went to see Edward on the tradesman's door down the hall.

'Edward, you need to pull the security gate closed at the back,' I said. Then I explained, in as much detail as I could, what had happened at the front of the shop.

'This is a joke, right?' Edward said. 'You shop girls have got a very strange sense of humour.'

'No, it is deadly serious. Please, let's just lock up then you can go and see Mr Levy and I'm sure he'll confirm what I've said.'

Edward opened the back door and we came face to face with Judd Butler.

'Miss Lightfoot, I just couldn't stay away.'

'Oh my goodness, Mr Butler!' I grabbed his arm and brought him inside.

As Edward pulled the grille shut and began to lock up he noticed that a group of people were gathering in the back alley.

'Kat, are these the folks you were talking about?' Edward asked.

I looked out and nodded. They were standing as though they were puppets whose strings had been cut. They were also in varying states of disarray, and there was blood on some of their faces and hands. My eyes fell on one of them wearing a fireman's uniform. His eyes had that blank, but somewhat evil glow. He shuffled from one foot to the other, then began to move with deliberate intent towards the door.

'Close the door quickly before they get eager.'

Edward did as I asked him. Then I led Judd into the kitchen, where he came face to face with Sylvia for the first time in five years.

'I think this gentleman could also do with some tea,' I said.

Sylvia looked up and her face flushed red when she saw Judd. 'Susie,' Judd said, stepping towards her.

Sylvia staggered back against a table and held her hand up in front of her to stop him from embracing her. 'No. No. I don't know you,' she said.

Judd stopped and fell to his knees. His voice was

pitiful. 'Please, Susie. I've come to take you home.'

Sylvia looked up at me horrified. 'You! This is *your* fault. Why did you bring him in here?'

I shook my head and backed out of the room, leaving them to settle their own affairs.

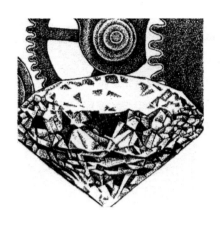

Ten

I went upstairs to see if Martin was all right. I found him working on yet another handgun. I sent all the workshop girls downstairs to talk to Mr Levy – they needed to know what was happening.

'Kat, look at this,' Martin said, proudly showing me the handgun. This one had been adapted to have an extra magazine on the top. 'Simple, but effective.'

'Could you teach me to use that?' I said, my mind taken up with a sudden need to be able to defend myself.

'Sure,' said Martin.

I was surprised that Martin agreed so readily, but then he didn't treat me like the other girls who worked at Tiffany's. I think this was because I was always very interested in his creations and tried to understand the technology behind his machines.

'We could go out to a quiet part of Central Park at the

weekend,' Martin said.

'Erm … I mean *now*,' I said. 'Can you show me now? I need to know how to use this weapon today.'

Martin frowned, so I explained what was happening outside. After I had finished, he went to the window and looked down onto Fifth Avenue. I joined him there, even though I wasn't sure I would like what I saw.

Below, the wedding party was still gathered, but now their clothing was even more blood-splattered, and if I leaned out a little I could see the groom still crouched by the door right below us. He was nursing the veil of his now dead bride. He appeared to be frozen or hypnotised, and the horde just stood there and stared at the building as though this was the focus their empty souls needed to help them return to their former humanity. Somehow I knew that this was impossible. These people had changed beyond recognition and beyond any help.

'It's been building to this,' I said. 'The last few days … there were clues and I saw them but just didn't understand what had to be done. Even my cat knew what these things were before I did.'

'It's a sickness, perhaps,' said Martin.

I shook my head.

'A fever of some sort, a poison like cholera.'

'This is nothing like cholera,' I said. 'The dead have returned from the grave.'

I realised that it was impossible to say that without a doom-laden timbre entering your voice. I felt like some sort of armageddon peddler.

'You can't know that.' Martin was too practical to believe in such things.

'I know what I'm saying is impossible. Maybe the darkness has touched me too in some way, but I can see what these things are, Martin. They are the stuff of nightmares.'

'Even if that's true, there must be a way to destroy them.'

'Spinetti's driver put a bullet in the brain of the bride,' I explained. 'And the soldier did the same to his fiancée's chaperone when she turned on them. It seemed to work, but it took several bullets to finish the job. Even then, I wasn't sure that the chaperone had really died. It was all so sudden and horrible. I really didn't understand what I was seeing.'

I rubbed my brow, feeling a headache coming on as my mind tried to focus and analyse everything I'd seen over the last few days. There was a clue there ... something that could help save us perhaps. If this group of people had changed so quickly during a wedding service, what had been the contributing factor? Perhaps it was witchcraft. I thought about the darkness that had hovered around the others I had seen, and the way Mr Pepper had been wary of the trees near the church, but I still couldn't put the puzzle together.

'Voodoo ...' Martin said suddenly as though reading my mind. 'Those goddamn Creoles ... This is how the South plans to win the war.'

'But … the Mayor declared New York an independent city. Technically we're not on any side, even though some of our boys have …'

'I know. But what better place to infiltrate the North?' Martin said.

I was horrified that our city might be used this way. It was a terrifying thought that we could all be subjected to some kind of witchcraft. Part of me didn't believe it though.

'If the South is to blame, then why would they turn their own soldiers?' I asked.

Martin looked at me sharply. 'You're right. They wouldn't.'

The work girls were gathered on the floor behind the counters in the main shop as Martin and I came downstairs. I nodded to them. For once, Lizzie and Agnes were quiet. All the workshop girls looked scared, and it reminded me that I should be feeling afraid too. I wasn't frightened though. I believed it was important to keep strong and upbeat. Giving up would only allow whatever evil had taken those poor people, to get to us too.

Levy and Rocky were still watching the door while Edward and Danny jointly kept an eye on the trade entrance. Sylvia was nowhere to be seen, so I left Martin to talk to Levy and went back to the kitchen to find her.

Sylvia was seated on one of the chairs when I came in and Judd was on his knees, head in her lap.

'I can't come back with you Judd. I never loved you and I didn't want to be married to you. My daddy made me.'

'I don't understand,' said Judd. 'I gave you everything. Then one day you up and left.'

'My life is here ...' Sylvia said. She met my eyes as I stood by the door. They held a silent plea.

'Mr Butler,' I said. 'Sylvia has said all she can right now. There are a lot of strange things going on outside and I know that all of us want to get out of here and back to our families.'

'What about the children?' Judd said. 'What about our kids, Susie?'

Sylvia shook her head and stroked his forehead. 'Judd, they are your kids.' She looked up at me. 'I never had any, and I didn't want a life of looking out for some dead woman's brood. It wasn't the living I wanted.' She pushed Judd away gently. 'I have to make tea.'

Judd remained on the floor. He seemed a broken man. I helped Sylvia make the tea, and once it was done I placed a cup down on the table near Judd.

'Look, Mr Butler, this isn't the time for this. When this whole thing is done, you and Syl ... Susie can find time to talk it through. But I'd appreciate it if, when we go into the other room, you don't say anything to the people in there about your relationship.'

Sylvia's water-filled eyes blinked and met mine. She mouthed 'Thank you', and I nodded to her to show I understood.

'This stuff is private, right enough,' said Judd.

'It is. And it's no-one's business but your own. So please … you'll just go along with the explanation I give for you, won't you?'

Judd nodded.

'Come on then. Let's go into the shop.'

Judd followed me meekly as Sylvia and I carried trays of teacups into the room.

'This is Mr Butler. Edward and I rescued him from those … things outside. He's in shock right now, so no-one bother him, okay?'

I sat Judd in the opposite corner from Marlene, who stopped looking at her nails just long enough to glance over at him. I made sure he was as far away from Levy as I could manage. Then Sylvia and I went around with tea for everyone.

'My Mother always prescribes this for shock,' I said to Marlene when she looked dubiously at the cup of brown liquid. 'Milk and sugar?'

'I brought my own mixer.' With that, Marlene picked up her skirt and pulled a small silver flask out of her garter. The workshop girls giggled as she poured a large tipple into the cup of tea. 'That should make it just about drinkable.'

Marlene certainly had an edge to her, but her unconventional behaviour had broken the tension in the room. I found myself smiling at her.

I looked around to see Rocky gazing back at her with real love in his eyes. Maybe he had only been in the store to buy her an engagement ring. I wasn't sure though. You see, I had already worked out what it meant when Levy called Rocky a *gonif*. It meant he was a thief, because I had heard him use the expression before when he was reading in his newspaper about someone who had robbed the bank on Sixth.

Rocky met my eyes, and I blushed because he had caught me watching him. Then he turned his eyes back to the door and raised the blind a little to look outside.

'This is ridiculous. We should just go out and blast a hole in them,' Rocky said. 'Several holes.'

'*Oy vey*! You can't kill innocent people,' Levy said. 'There could be some of my customers out there.'

'There's nothing innocent about these folks,' Rocky said. 'Marlene … come hold this gun while I drink some tea.'

Marlene took the gun like an expert, much to the titillation of the workshop girls, while Rocky sat down in her chair and sedately drank his tea as though he were taking a break – which I suppose was exactly what he was doing.

Maude and Lizzie whispered to each other, and whatever the girls were saying went rapidly down the line to end with Agnes, who erupted in a brief burst of stifled giggles.

'You get some tea,' Rocky said to Levy when he took

up point again, retrieving the gun from Marlene. 'And just for the record, I'm no criminal. I made my money in good old fashioned gold.'

Levy had the good grace to blush, but he soon forgot his embarrassment when a barrage of gunfire sounded right outside the shop and the dead horde began to yell and moan.

'There's someone out there!' I gasped. I threw myself on the door, pulling up the blind, and that's when I saw Mr Pepper fighting his way through the ghoulish wedding party. He was using his cane to hit away the grasping fingers of the creatures.

'Open up!' he yelled. 'For God sake let me in.'

I yanked the bolt back and began to pull the door open.

'What are you doing?' Rocky said.

'That's Mr Pepper. We can't leave him out there.'

Though clearly shaken, Levy helped me unlock the grille. Pepper was in close combat with what I thought might be the bride's father. The dead man was snapping at him with razor-sharp, yellowed teeth, but somehow Pepper kept him at bay. He hit the man hard between the eyes with the silver cat's head on the top of his cane.

'Help him!' I implored Rocky, and he aimed his gun at Pepper's attacker, shooting him in the leg. The walking corpse, as I was now coming to believe they were, fell and let go of Mr Pepper, giving him an opportunity to run towards the door. A uniformed officer ran forward and tackled Pepper to the ground. Levy rushed out in an uncharacteristic surge of bravery. He grabbed the officer, pulling him away.

'Officer! He's not one of *them*,' Levy started to say, but the policeman turned on him, and Levy discovered, much to his detriment, that the officer *was* 'one of them'. The officer's teeth connected with Levy's arm and bit into him, worrying his flesh, through his jacket, like a vicious dog.

Pepper slammed the butt of his gun into the officer's face. His jaws tore away, taking a chunk of Levy's jacket with him as he fell to the ground. Rocky shot at a few more of the horde as they began to bear down on Pepper and Levy. Then, the other creatures turned and fell upon the new corpses. It helped to distract them and gave Pepper time to run inside, dragging Levy with him. I closed and locked the grille behind them with trembling fingers, while Rocky continued to fire into the crowd.

We closed the inner door and I saw Sylvia holding Levy as he slumped against the counter.

'Are you injured?' asked Pepper.

'That *dreck* bit me!' Levy said.

'Let me see the wound,' Pepper said. 'Hold this for me, please.' He held out the cane and I took it. I couldn't help noticing the wet blood that had seeped into all of the lines carved into the cat's face. I avoided touching it for fear of contamination.

Levy let Pepper examine his arm. 'He's broken the

skin, but not much. It's more that he marked you through your clothing I think. Would have to take your shirt off to be certain. But that was very fortunate.'

'Thank goodness,' Sylvia said. 'Come into the back and I'll clean the wound.'

'You should disinfect it as well,' Pepper said. 'Has anyone got any liquor?'

All eyes turned to Marlene, who innocently continued to examine her nails.

Eleven

Martin began to bring his weapons and spare magazines downstairs, but not before he strapped the metal tank containing the diamond off-cut bullets onto my back.

'This is the safety,' he said pointing to a small copper switch on the side of the gun. 'This is not the best way to learn about weapons, so I hope you have a good memory.'

He talked me through how the Remington fired, showing me how to aim it. I looked down the sight and listened to his explanation of how the trigger worked.

'Don't you want to wear this?' I said.

'No. I think you'll need it more than me. This gun will rely less on accuracy and more on sheer volume. Just don't press the trigger when anyone *alive* is in the way.'

I smiled at his sudden acceptance of my theory that the crazies outside were all dead.

I practised aiming as he wound up the mechanism on

the bullet tank. 'This won't start to work until you remove the safety and fire the first bullet. When you release the trigger the mechanism and the weapon will both stop.'

We went back downstairs into the shop and Martin gave out guns to all of the men. Marlene was the only other female he gave a gun to. This one was an unmodified rifle, but he had seen the way she had handled Rocky's handgun and I think he realised that she knew her way around weapons. He had the same respect for and trust in her that he did me, although I felt that Marlene probably knew far more about life than I ever would. When he began to describe how the rifle worked, Marlene winked at him and cracked open the long barrel expertly.

'I got this covered already,' she smiled.

I was now in awe of her, as were Lizzie, Agnes and the other workshop girls.

Sylvia came back in the room when Martin was showing me how to reload the tank with fresh bullets. He had brought down boxes and boxes of them and had placed them on the counters.

'That's quite an arsenal,' Rocky said.

'How's Mr Levy?' I asked, and Sylvia glanced guiltily at Judd.

'He's okay. I washed the wound. It's very bruised but fortunately not much breaking of the skin, as you said.'

'Right. Let's hope it's going to be okay,' I said.

'Why wouldn't it be okay?' Sylvia asked, panic colouring her cheeks. 'He's going to be fine, isn't he?'

I noticed Judd watching us and thought carefully about how to respond. 'I'm sure he will be fine, Sylvia. And I'm sure he's very concerned about his wife right now too.'

Sylvia caught herself. 'Yes. He said he was just now actually …'

I was worried about Mother and Sally also. They had been on my mind ever since the siege on Tiffany's began. What were they doing right now? Was Mother sitting in her workroom, sewing up a skirt or jacket for a customer? Was Sally playing in the yard with Holly? Panic overwhelmed me at the thought of Sally outside, playing, and another of these things stumbling their way into the back yard. I began to wish I had told Mother what was happening.

There was a sharp thump on the grille. Then another. Then the whole wall of shutters shook as the creatures began to hammer on them with their fists.

'What's happening?' asked Rocky.

'They have just decided they are going to try to get inside. They don't usually do that,' Pepper explained.

'What do you mean *usually*?' I shouted over the din. 'I think you'd better tell us exactly what you know.'

Pepper turned those pale blue eyes on me and I realised that my first guess had been right. He knew much more about these things than he had initially let on.

The afternoon had turned into evening and the workshop girls had all retired upstairs to find a place to sleep. Those of us with weapons were taking sleep shifts. The banging on the shutters had stopped after about half an hour and we were left, poised, waiting for a full-on attack. With the fear of imminent danger, the others forgot the conversation we'd had with Pepper. But I wasn't going to let him get away with not telling me what he knew. Even if he thought the truth would scare me. Nothing could scare me more than my own imagination right then. Facts and real insight into the creatures could save our lives and I wasn't going to let this one go.

The grandfather clock in the corner of the shop struck one. All was eerily quiet outside as though the creatures themselves were merely windup toys that had run down.

Pepper and I were the only ones awake. Levy was sleeping in the kitchen and Sylvia had taken to the stockroom. When Judd had tried to follow her, I had pulled him aside again and pointed out once more that this wasn't the time to settle their differences. He had conceded and curled up behind one of the counters and rapidly fallen asleep.

'Why did they stop?' I asked Pepper.

'I'm not sure. As I said, the attempt to get inside was unusual. They often wait for their prey to fall into their hands. Usually by then the person has lost all of their will to survive. They've given up.'

'You have to tell me everything,' I said. 'Don't leave

anything out. You won't be saving my female sensibilities, you'll just be patronising me, Mr Pepper.'

Pepper nodded and then began to tell me the strangest tale I had ever heard.

'I was in the first wave of soldiers to sign up to the war effort,' Pepper began. 'We'd been marching south for some time when we first noticed the darkness.'

I suppressed a gasp on hearing these words, because I didn't want him to think I couldn't take the truth. Even so, I was shocked at Pepper's use of the word 'darkness', because it was exactly what I had come to believe was somehow in the creatures.

'One night when we were camping not far from the Mississippi, I had a strange dream. I imagined that something was out there in the trees and it came from a place that I could only describe as *darkness*. I woke up abruptly and thought I had been screaming in my sleep, because I could feel this terrible fear clutching my chest. I was gasping for breath and my heart was racing. Then I heard it. The scream hadn't been a residue of the dream: it was real. A man was yelling, and I knew then it was the night watch.

'I ran from my tent and, sure enough, some wild thing had attacked the boy that the Colonel had left on patrol duty. He was dead before we reached him. But whatever had gotten to him had fled when the camp roused.

'The boy's name was Trevor Davies and he was only 19. His body was … torn at. But I don't need to describe it to know that you understand me. You saw already what those things do …' Pepper said, then he continued without waiting for my acknowledgement.

'We buried him the next morning, and I remember writing a letter that would go back to his family. It said that he had died in the line of duty and nothing more. The Colonel thought it best if his parents believed he had died a hero. And why not? That poor kid. Had he ever seen battle, he was likely to have been among the first casualties anyway.

'A few nights later, and in yet another camp, I heard one of the patrol guards yelling. My heart was pounding when I ran out to see what the commotion was. I saw the two men on patrol aiming their weapons at a man standing on the perimeter of the camp. "What's going on here?" the Colonel said, coming out of his tent. Then he stopped and stared at the man. From where I was I couldn't see him, but I could see the Colonel's face, and he looked like he had seen a ghost.

'Something made me step forward, and then I saw for myself. It was Trevor Davies! He was alive, and he looked like he had pulled himself directly from the grave. "I'm hungry," he said, turning his head towards me. "Pepper, feed me."

'I backed away and the Colonel ordered his men to open fire. Davies just smiled as the bullets hit him. They pumped so much lead into him that he should have died of poisoning even if the holes didn't kill him. But he just stood there and took the bullets. Then one of the solders kind of lost it. He ran at Davies, and this time he fired point blank into the dead boy's head. The boy fell and he stayed down. The doctor examined him and amputated his head for good measure. We buried him for the second time, and none of us spoke of it again until some weeks later when we were marching towards our first confrontation with the enemy just outside New Orleans.'

Pepper paused as though he needed to catch his breath. His words terrified me but I wanted him to go on. I had to hear the rest.

'We passed through miles of open fields that were flanked by trees, and at the other end, when our final destination was almost in sight, we found dense brush. Our scout team had told us that the enemy lay just beyond. "We'll settle here for the night," the Colonel said. "Try to get some sleep, boys. Tomorrow we become heroes." But I think, under normal circumstances, we would have pushed ahead then and there. I saw the Colonel's face when he glanced into the gloomy woods. He didn't want to pass through there as the night fell, and I knew what it was that frightened him so much.

'I was on guard duty that evening with another soldier by the name of Paulson. He was a bit of a joker, liked to play pranks, so when he went missing I just thought he was fooling around. But when the next shift came on, Paulson still hadn't returned, so I sounded the alert and a few soldiers began to search the area for him. That's when I saw the darkness in the real world: until then, I had seen it only in my nightmares. It was gathering in the woods around us, like a dark cloud waiting for us to walk right in and breathe it in. All that evil.

'Paulson was never found and the Colonel declared him a deserter. We went on to battle the next day and won our first minor victory. But that evening I noticed that a few of the soldiers had developed dry coughs, and later a few of them became sick with fever. I started to write a journal after that. I felt this urge to chronicle what was happening. Not just the war, but the strange behaviour of some of the men.

'The sickness delayed our march to rendezvous with the main army and Major Simpson. We stayed at the new camp on the site our enemy had previously held for a few days extra, but the sick men didn't get any better. "It's some kinda swamp fever," one of the doctors said. Then Colonel Jackson decided we couldn't stay any longer, so we left the sick behind with one of the field doctors and a few fit soldiers who would bring them on to the meeting point when they recovered. Then we marched forward and on to New Orleans.

'We never saw those men again. Or the doctor. And when the Colonel sent back a small scout team to find out what was happening, none of them returned either.

'By the time we rejoined the main army, our troops were seriously diminished. Men had been going missing all along the way. The strange thing was, we were never attacked in our tents. It was only those who braved stepping outside of the camp at night that were never seen again.

'Colonel Jackson was pulled up in front of Major Simpson and it looked like he would be court-martialed, because the Major didn't like what the Colonel said about how he had lost so many men. He didn't believe in the darkness, you see. He thought that the Colonel was incompetent and was merely making excuses. Finally I went to the Major and told him all I'd seen. "That's nonsense, Pepper!" he yelled at me. "But I admire your loyalty to the Colonel." I tried to persuade him that I was telling the truth, but he wouldn't listen. He even accused me of having some sort of mental instability. This made me furious. I called the Major an idiot and caused a massive row.

During the argument, a soldier rode in at breakneck speed and started yelling to see the Major. The man was brought in and the Major instantly forgot I was there as the soldier began to pour out a tale about how his entire troop had been lost. This soldier had also seen the darkness and it was preying on his soul, just as much as it was mine. When he too called it by that name I found the Major staring at me. The truth of my words was finally sinking in.

'The Major had no choice but to believe the Colonel after that or else accept that we were *all* crazy – and that wasn't a scenario he was willing to recognise. He needed all the men he had to face the next battle. So the Colonel was reinstated and we all pushed forward to try and take New Orleans.

'We moved up the Mississippi, and a few more of the men fell to the mysterious swamp fever, but it didn't stop our troops. Eventually Flag Officer David Farragut led an assault, and by 25 April, we were occupying New Orleans.

'I don't want to talk about the battle, or the men I killed, but I was among the wounded. By then, many men had died from injuries when left untreated. The Colonel had us patched up the best the field doctors could do, then they sent us home to recover.

'When I got back, I told one of the doctors what I had seen. I didn't realise it, but my honesty saved me from having to return. They discharged me on grounds of mental instability. It wasn't the way I would have liked to leave the army, but you see, unless you touch the darkness it is a hard thing to believe in.'

I didn't know what to say to Pepper, but his story struck such profound terror into my soul, not least because of the similarities of the dream that continued to haunt me, but also because I couldn't help remembering that my brother, Henry, was still out there.

Was the darkness surrounding Henry and his troop even now?

Twelve

Rocky and Judd had taken over the watch half way through the night, but I had struggled to fall asleep. I was very concerned about Mother and Sally. Even if this hadn't touched our street, Mother would be frantic with worry because I had not returned. So, I tossed and turned, trying to get comfortable on the shop floor until finally, just before dawn, I managed to slip into a fitful sleep for a few hours with my head resting on the copper bullet tank.

Every little noise disturbed me. When the grandfather clock struck seven I pulled myself up from the floor, stretched, and strapped the tank back onto my back.

I went into the kitchen to make some tea, only to find Levy and Sylvia in a compromising position. They were lying on the floor, Levy on top of Sylvia. Her skirts were up over her thighs and Levy was rocking back and forth between her legs, his bare bottom peeking out from under his shirt, while his breeches were down around his ankles.

'Woah!' I said.

Levy pulled himself free, stood up and began to button his breeches, but by then I'd already seen too much.

I closed the door quickly, hoping that Judd was still sleeping in the shop, and turned back to them as Sylvia pulled her pantaloons back up and straightened her dress down over her legs.

'We could die,' said Sylvia, buttoning up her blouse. 'I think you should know Gerald and I love each other.'

'Sylvia, Mr Levy, I know that you have feelings for each other. It's been obvious to me for a while. But now is not the time to … express that affection. Sylvia … you *know* why.'

Sylvia had the good grace to blush. I bustled around ignoring them while I placed the kettle on the stove. It gave them both ample opportunity to neaten themselves as much as possible.

'I'll send the girls down to help distribute the tea,' I said to Sylvia, but it was more a warning that she and Levy should behave themselves right now in case anyone else came in. Then I took two cups and went out of the room.

Martin was watching the growing group of men and women from the window of his work room.

'Here,' I said, holding out the tea cup.

He took the cup between both of his hands and I looked down into the street.

The shop was surrounded, ten rows deep, by the walking dead. Did this mean that these things were everywhere, and not just surrounding the shop? It certainly appeared to be the case. I felt panic rising in my throat but swigged my tea to hide the anxiety from Martin. I didn't want him to think of me as a weak, screaming female, because I knew that if he continued to believe I was strong then I would be.

'I was doing some thinking last night,' Martin said. 'Once, I read a book about witchcraft and superstitions.'

'I'm not even going to ask why you would have such a book, Martin … but, go on.'

'These things could be *zonbi*.'

'Zom-what?'

'*Zonbi*. Superstition has them as the dead who are risen by the magic of a voodoo priest. Africans brought this magic with them when we stole them from their country and made them slaves.'

'You're determined to blame the Creoles for this, aren't you?'

'There has to be an explanation for this, even an illogical one,' Martin said. 'You see, I don't believe in magic, but I look out there and I see something that just shouldn't be happening.'

'Martin, why haven't the police cleared the streets by now? Why hasn't any help arrived at all?' I asked, although I already knew the answer. I just didn't want to admit it.

'It's widespread. Perhaps everywhere,' he said, confirming my worst fears. 'But that doesn't mean that help isn't out there.'

Martin sipped his tea. I had taken to adding sugar to every cup now to give us energy. We weren't going to get any food, anytime soon, not unless the army suddenly decided to turn up and rescue us, so I was already thinking ahead on the practicalities of our survival. It was what kept me sane.

'One of us is going to have to try to go out and find that help,' Martin said, as though he were reading my mind.

'That would be suicide.'

'Starvation is what eventually faces us if we don't try. That's just supposing we can hold them off indefinitely.'

'We have water,' I said.

'Yes. And we can live on that for a while. Maybe even weeks. But not forever.'

I shook my head as though to deny the obvious truth, but I felt fear and anxiety tighten their grip on my mind and soul. I felt like I couldn't breathe, and terror rose in my throat and threatened to suffocate me. I likened it to the sensation of wearing your corset too tight. My ribs and chest heaved but seemed to get no air at all. Should we sit this out for weeks? Perhaps then the creatures would get tired and leave? Somehow I didn't think this would happen. They looked as though they planned to stay until we came out, or until, tired of this waiting game, they descended on us and finally broke through the shutters.

The thought of this gave me the intense belief that I was having some kind of premonition. Or maybe it was just accepting the inevitability of our situation.

'Are you okay?' asked Martin.

I expelled a breath sharply and nodded. 'I can't stand the thought of losing anyone to this. But I know you're right. We can't sit this out and wait for them to come in after us. We're trapped and we need an exit. We have to talk to the others.'

I went downstairs again and, after a final glance out of the window at the things below, Martin followed. In the shop, everyone was up and about and Levy had gathered them all to have a meeting.

'I'm going to try to get help …' Martin said, coming into the room. 'It's the only thing we can do. Everyone has to sit tight. I'll try to sneak away via the trade exit. That may be the only opportunity we have to get the police here.'

'No, that won't do at all,' said Pepper. 'If we are to escape, then we all go together and we fight our way out.'

'Are you crazy?' Agnes cried. 'We can't go outside with them.'

The workshop girls began to wail and cry then. Maude was sobbing uncontrollably on Hermione's shoulder, while Emily and Lizzie chattered on about how they just *couldn't* go outside. I suddenly realised how privileged we had been when they were shocked into silence.

'Shut it!' Marlene said firmly, and the girls stopped their noise immediately. 'If we gotta fight then there's no point whining about it. It's fight or die, and I for one don't fancy sitting here any longer. Let's kick some cannibal ass.'

'*Cannibal*,' wailed Lizzie, and this set the girls off crying again. This time louder and harder than before.

'Well what the fuck do you wanna call them?' Marlene said. Her calm exterior was beginning to crack.

'*Zonbis*,' said Martin.

The screaming girls were finally silenced when a crash came from the corridor leading to the hallway. They cowered behind the counter, holding each other, eyes wide with fright. Martin, Pepper and I were the first through the door as the noise of gunfire filled the enclosed air around us and made me wince with pain.

We found that the zombies had decided to bring the fight to us after all. Several of the walking dead were already in the corridor and Danny and Edward, with their backs to us, were firing into the approaching crowd.

Martin opened fire with his new, compact Remington.

'Take off the safety, Kat,' he yelled in between shots. 'Everybody duck down.'

My fingers wouldn't work at first. I pressed the safety button, then pulled back on the hammer, but realised I had done it all in the wrong order somehow. I saw Martin glance at me, heard him yell again, but by then I could barely hear because of the deafening gunfire.

I raised the gun with shaking fingers, 'Get down!' I shouted, and as Edward and Danny threw themselves aside I squeezed the trigger. A hail of bullets poured out of the narrow barrel with impossible speed.

Shocked by the power of the gun as it pushed back into my body, I released the trigger. The gun stopped firing and I watched the damage happen as the bullets found their mark. It was as though time had slowed down.

The two zombies at the front were propelled backwards into the others as the bullets pummelled into them. One of the bullets hit a male in the mouth, smashing through his teeth, and ruptured inside his head. The diamond off-cuts ricocheted out into the creatures behind. The first to fall was a female in a waitress costume who caught a diamond shard in the eye. It passed straight through, glutinous jelly bursting from the socket, and she tumbled forward as the shard burrowed into her brain.

The falling bodies weakened the initial onslaught, and the zombies behind paused as though they feared death. Then the next row fell on the first and a fight broke out among them as they scrabbled to get to the blood and meat of the truly dead. The bodies were dragged backwards into the small area that Edward usually occupied, where the hungry mob waited. We were then faced with yet another row of them, who started to stagger down the corridor towards us once more.

I stared down the sight of the gun at black, swirling, evil-filled eyes, then opened fire once more.

This time I was prepared for the recoil, and I sprayed the approaching zombies with bullets.

More of the creatures fell as the bullets powered into them, splitting on impact and sending shards of diamond off-cuts into and through their bodies, and then into the creatures behind them.

The corridor was like a slaughterhouse as I stepped forward over the fallen dead. Blood and gore covered the floor and ran down the walls. The creatures started to move back as I advanced. I could see that there were only a handful of them still moving.

I fired intermittent bursts at them, and the zombies reacted by backing away still further.

The zombies looked confused. They were drawn to the bodies around them, ripping viciously with hooked fingers at the mounds of bloody flesh while simultaneously shoving the gore into their gobbling mouths. They were so preoccupied with eating that they almost instinctively dragged their food behind them as they left the corridor, passed Edward's table and exited by the rear door.

Levy and Danny came up behind me and wrestled the table up, using it as a barricade to propel the final zombies out into the alley. When the room was clear, Pepper pushed the breached door back in place and ran the bolt. *It was undamaged.*

I holstered the gun, which was feeling warm in my hand, taking care to put the safety back on. This thing could do a lot of damage. I felt powerful. Invincible. And I was looking around me, wondering why everyone had such sour faces. We could fight these things. We really could. Our first battle had been won.

'How did they get in?' asked Pepper. 'Who opened the grille?'

'We don't know,' said Edward, glancing at Danny. 'I went for a bathroom break. Danny went to talk to his boss. We left Judd behind to watch the door.'

'Where is Judd?' I asked, my gun-toting elation suddenly subsiding.

We searched the building.

'You take the washrooms,' Levy said to Marlene and me. 'Martin, you check your own level. I'll check the top three floors.'

'I'll go with you,' said Martin.

'No. It's off-limits to employees. You know that.'

'Well there's no time for that nonsense now,' said Pepper. 'Take Martin with you.'

I saw Danny exchange a look with Rocky and wondered again about the origins of Rocky's wealth, but I was curious about the upper floors now too.

I went with Marlene and Rocky to check every room on the ground level. Levy and Martin were gone some time, but we all convened back in the shop eventually.

'That crazy old man went out there,' said Rocky. 'He's a gonner for sure.'

'Come to think of it, he looked pretty upset this morning,' said Marlene, who was proving to be very observant despite her appearance of indifference. 'He went to the kitchen to get a glass of water, but he came back without one. He looked all sad and serious and I just put it down to … you know … there being man-eating monsters outside and all.'

Sylvia burst into tears. 'I can't take this anymore!'

I put my arm around her and led her to a chair while trying to ignore the curiosity of the workshop girls.

But there was no escaping the zombies. The banging and rattling began again. A new fury seemed to have taken hold of them, and I knew that they were determined to get inside one way or the other.

'How long do you think those shutters will hold?' asked Lizzie.

No-one answered. We didn't want to speculate.

'Why won't they just stop that?' cried Maude, bursting into another round of tears. She was really getting on my nerves.

'I'll get you some water,' I said to Sylvia.

'She don't want that,' said Marlene, holding out the flask. 'Here. This will cheer you up.'

I opened the flask, sniffed it and held it to Sylvia's lips. I couldn't help thinking how fortunate this all was for her, in one sense. There was no more unwanted husband hanging around now that Judd was gone. But I tried to shake the notion away and give her sympathy. It was a cruel thought and most unlike me. After all, Judd may have looked like some sweet old man, but how was I to know what it had been like for her to be married off to him at such a young age? She sipped at the flask, swallowed, then coughed as she choked at the harsh taste.

'See, the colour is back in her cheeks already,' laughed Marlene. 'That's Jamaican rum. The best there is!'

Thirteen

'We have tremendous firepower with Martin's weapons,' I pointed out.

'There are hundreds of them out there. We'd never break through,' said Rocky. 'And believe me, if I thought we could do a runner then you'd not see my heels for dust.'

Martin had taken the regular guns from Rocky and Danny and had spent the whole day in his workshop adapting them using materials that he had to hand.

'This one,' he said, raising Rocky's gun, 'is now a dialight. It will cut through metal. I know this because I used it to cut diamonds, and diamond is the hardest substance there is.'

'Dialight? Show me what it does,' Rocky said.

Martin took him upstairs to the workshop. I followed, because I was curious to see what new creations he had come up with.

'You'll need to wear these. This does get a little bright,' Martin said, passing each of us a pair of tinted spectacles.

Once our eyes were protected, he pointed Rocky's gun at a sheet of flattened metal and squeezed the trigger. Instead of the loud retort of a bullet being ejected from the nozzle, a bright light ran from an extra barrel that Martin had added to the original. The beam hit the metal and a hole melted immediately in the middle of the sheet.

'But how does it work?' asked Rocky. 'That's a light isn't it? How can light *burn*?'

He went over to the metal sheet and raised his finger to poke at the hole.

'I wouldn't, if I were you,' warned Martin. 'It's red hot.'

Rocky held his palm above the hole and nodded. 'I can feel the heat.'

'There's a flaw, unfortunately,' said Martin. 'This gun will work only during the daytime. It needs natural light. Look here. This is a small mirror that's angled to pick up light. The light is fed into the tube and reflects through the diamond inside.

'Diamond?' Rocky said.

'They aren't just fashion accessories, you know. Diamonds deserve a lot of respect; they are amazing things. Anyway, that's why it's called a dialight. Diamond light. The reflected light is intensified as it travels through the diamond. It becomes so bright that it heats up. It is like harnessing the Sun, if you like.'

'Where did you learn to do all this, kid?'

'From my father, Crichton Crewe, but most people of worth called him Herr Doktor. He was a scientist and an inventor. He taught me his art from an early age. I've just taken it to a new level. But without him, I wouldn't have had the skills to make these things. Or the knowledge.'

We were all suitably impressed by the thought of Herr Doktor and his marvellous inventions, and even Rocky's questions were silenced for a while as we pondered the magnificence of the dialight.

'Any questions?' Martin said.

'One thing did occur to me. Why doesn't the light melt the barrel as it passes through it?' I asked.

'Well observed, Kat,' Martin said. 'Because it's lined with diamond shards that just reflect the energy back into itself. Feel this ... the barrel doesn't even get hot when it's used.'

I had to give it to Martin, the gun was good, but it was unfortunately not much use at night, which was why, with a flick of a switch, the dialight could be turned back into an ordinary handgun. It still contained the diamond-shard bullets, too, and I knew first-hand what damage they could do.

'It occurred to me that the diamond shards make good debris inside the bullet heads. Kat's use of them yesterday proved that they do a lot more damage than regular bullets. So, from now on, you'll load your guns with these.' Martin handed each of us a handful of bullets;

all were different, according to the calibre of the weapons we had. 'But use them wisely,' he warned. 'We don't have many left, and making them takes time.'

That was when I got the idea to start production again in the workshop. Only this time the girls would not be making jewellery, but bullets under Martin's expert direction.

The silence, when it came, was more deafening than the constant battering of the grilles and doors. It was so uncanny that I had to go back upstairs just to look out at the zombies again and assure myself that they were still there.

The creatures had backed away from the building. They resembled a crowd who had just calmly exited a church. Some were looking at the door, patiently waiting for us to open up, while others had turned to face each other as though they were having a conversation. I couldn't see any lips moving, however, so I thought that this must mean they had gone into some type of trance.

'Why have they stopped? And why was it that the effort they made to get inside seemed so ... indifferent?' I said.

The thought occurred to me that they were doing what we expected them to do, rather than what they really *wanted* to do.

'There is more going on here than we understand,' Martin said, joining me at the window.

At that moment the collective turned and looked upwards towards us as though they knew we were discussing them in Martin's workshop. It was eerie, and Martin even took a step backwards as the creatures' eyes fell on him.

Then I heard a sound, quiet at first but increasing in volume as more zombies joined in.

'Martin. Martin. Martin,' the zombies chanted.

'What on Earth …?' I whispered.

I turned to find Levy standing in the doorway of Martin's workroom. It was growing late and the room was full of shadows. I couldn't see Levy's face at first, but from the way he was standing, I had the distinct feeling that he was in some kind of trance. Just like the zombies.

'Martin …' he said.

Martin jumped and spun around. Levy stepped forward into the light. He looked hungry, but then none of us had eaten and the tea was rapidly running out.

My stomach churned as I felt compelled to watch Levy, watching Martin. I almost expected my boss to start chanting Martin's name.

'Mr Levy?' Martin said. 'Do you hear that?'

'Yes,' said Levy. He blinked, then looked around the workshop as though he were just seeing the room for the first time. 'Good work, Martin. Carry on.'

Levy left the room but my paranoia didn't. I looked at Martin to see if he had noticed Levy's weird behaviour, but he was looking out at the zombies again.

They were quiet again and once more facing the door as though they expected us to open up and let them in at any moment.

'They still have intelligence. Like a collective knowledge,' Martin said.

'That's impossible.'

'Not if the darkness is in them,' said Pepper, appearing at the door. 'I just saw Levy in the kitchen. He doesn't look good. I might need to see that bite again, and I'm wondering if you'll give me a hand if he goes … *strange*.'

I nodded. Pepper and I had a connection and it was almost as though he knew what I was thinking.

'What did you mean about the darkness being *in* them?' I asked.

Pepper looked over his shoulder at the girls working in the main workshop, then he came into the room and closed the door.

'I have been thinking about this a lot. The first man changed when he was attacked. None of us saw by what. But it was different for some of the others. They got sick and started to change after searching for Paulson. I don't know what's causing this phenomenon but I do know that it all ends up the same way. The people infected die and turn into those creatures. It's like they have lost their souls.'

'And yet they can reason, even though the logic is insane. I have heard them talk.'

'The old woman in the park?' Pepper said.

'Yes. And there was another man, too. They all say they are hungry and they all say …'

'It's getting dark …' said Levy, opening the workshop door.

I stopped speaking and stared at him.

'Another day has almost gone,' Levy continued. 'We really need to come up with a plan. I feel like we're talking in circles already.'

'I know,' said Pepper. 'Let's all go downstairs and see what everyone has decided.'

Levy turned and walked away again. I found myself looking into Pepper's eyes, and I was pretty certain that I knew what he was thinking.

'Go downstairs,' Pepper said. Then he turned to Martin. 'I need you to adapt something for me too.'

I left the room before I could learn what it was, but as I crossed the workshop I heard a grinding sound. I turned back to see the frame of the door illuminated. Martin was using the dialight one more time before the daylight disappeared.

Rocky, Danny and Marlene were deep in conversation when the four of us came down to the shop.

'I'm going stir-crazy here,' said Marlene.

'Pepper,' said Rocky. 'We've been talking. We think our only chance is to make a run for it.'

Pepper nodded. 'I think I'm coming to the same conclusion. We may have to just shoot our way through the mob and run.'

'It's as good a plan as any,' Levy said. 'Better than just sitting this out. If we men flank the women, have them in the middle of us, then hopefully we can get everyone out safely.'

I couldn't take my eyes off Levy. His colour was wrong. His skin looked damp and yellow in the decreasing light, yet he sounded fine.

'And go where?' asked Sylvia. 'How do we know how far this has spread? I mean, where are they coming from anyway?'

Her voice was rising in pitch and she seemed on the edge of hysteria.

'Sylvia,' Levy said. 'I'm so sorry about this. I just want to get you out of here and to safety. Then things are going to change. I promise you … and I'm sorry …'

Her eyes met his for a while. She didn't seem to notice that he wasn't looking well.

I looked away from them. I didn't want to think about what could happen beyond the door. I just wanted to get out of here and see if Mother and Sally were okay. Even so, I had to agree that Sylvia was right. We didn't know what lay beyond the horde and if there was anything left of the world outside to hide in.

'Okay. It's decided then,' Pepper said. 'We'll sit this night out and then we'll make a run for it tomorrow. We need to prepare the workshop girls for this, Kat. Can you do that? The last thing we need is a group of screaming women drawing the zombies down on us.'

I nodded. 'Sylvia will help me give them *the talk*. Won't you?' I said, taking her hand.

Sylvia rose to the occasion as I hoped she would, and she followed me upstairs to tell the girls what was happening.

On the stairs I realised that this was the first time we had been alone since Judd had disappeared. I felt her squeeze my hand.

'I can't imagine Judd falling into the hands of those creatures. It was suicide to go out like that.'

That was the point, of course. Judd had thrown himself into the lion's den and then left the gate open. I wasn't sure if the last part was by design or if he simply hadn't thought about it as he ran out. Maybe the zombies were crowding the door as he opened it. The thought of them catching hold of Judd and biting into him flashed in my mind. I gulped, feeling sick again. I had seen such horrors since all this began. Surely my imagination couldn't show me anything worse?

The girls took the news more calmly than I thought they would, though I didn't think any of us would get much sleep that night. Somehow it would have been better if we had made the decision and just gone straight for it. But I saw the sense in doing this in the morning rather than at night. The dark was crowding around the building like a thick miasma and it emanated from the creatures as they stood outside, swaying as though they were dancing to music that only they could hear.

'Let's try and get some rest,' I said. 'Tomorrow we're making a break for it, whatever happens.'

At that moment the banging started again. It made me wonder just what the zombies knew about our plan already and if they were determined to make sure we didn't get any sleep at all.

Fourteen

I woke to the sound of scraping. It was like nails on a slate board. I sat up, looked around the shop and began to wonder where everyone was. By instinct I strapped the bullet tank back in place on my back, checked the handgun and re-holstered it.

It was still dark outside but I could see perfectly because the gaslight flame was on low. No-one here wanted to sleep in the dark. It would have been too suffocating under the circumstances. I checked the grandfather clock. It was two in the morning. As I moved through the room, I saw Marlene and Rocky curled up next to each other and both sound asleep. They suited each other somehow. I hadn't realised that when I first met them.

I stopped moving because I didn't want to disturb them. *I probably just imagined the noise anyway*, I

149

thought.

I was about to try to settle down and go to sleep again when there was a loud creak outside. I looked towards the corridor. The door was closed. I assumed that Martin and the girls were upstairs sleeping, and Sylvia was probably curled up once more in the store room, but where was Edward? He should have been here monitoring the door, while Danny was supposed to be watching the back.

I reached the door and I stood and waited. Nothing. *I was imagining this!* Then. *There.*

My left hand turned the door knob, while my right held the gun tightly. The door opened silently; it was well maintained and the hinges where oiled regularly, so that our comings and goings into the shop should not distract our customers from their browsing. I glanced down into the corridor and saw Danny hunched against the back door, gun in hand, head down, sound asleep. Exhaustion, I supposed, had finally overcome any fear of the door being breached again. I looked the other way. The corridor was not as well lit as the shop. To my right there was a patch of shadow where the stairs to the upper rooms were. The arch lay in total darkness. The sight of it terrified me. Not least because the corridor still had signs of the zombie attack. The night made the darkening stains on the floors and walls seem all the more sinister. I crossed the corridor to the kitchen and was about to open the door when I saw Pepper coming towards me from the stairwell.

I heard the creaking sound again. Pepper pointed upwards. I felt less afraid of the dark in his company. I turned and silently followed him towards the stairs, and we went up as quietly as possible.

In the workshop, Agnes, Lizzie and the girls were sleeping – which was a minor miracle.

'This way,' Pepper whispered as he opened the door to Martin's workshop.

'What are you doing?' asked Martin. He was standing on the other side of the room near the other door.

'We heard something,' I said.

'Me too,' Martin said. 'But we can't go up there.'

'There are stairs behind that door,' I stated to myself rather than to them.

'Yes, but we *can't* go there,' Martin repeated.

'Why not?' Pepper asked.

'It's the diamond vaults and Mr Charles' office,' Martin explained. 'Even I'm not allowed up there.'

'But I thought you searched for Judd with Mr Levy?' Pepper said.

Martin shook his head. 'Levy searched alone. When we got up here he wouldn't let me go with him. He's my boss. What could I do?'

An uncomfortable feeling began to work its way up my spine. *Levy had searched for Judd alone.* Did Levy know that Judd was Sylvia's husband? What if Judd hadn't left the building? It seemed unlikely, though, because Judd had good reason to run away.

'Come on,' said Pepper, opening the door.

The scraping noise was louder as we reached the second floor, and I was now certain it was coming from another floor upstairs. It was like the sound of a rusty weathervane, only I knew the Tiffany's building didn't have one.

'I'll go first,' Pepper said, and Martin automatically took up the rear, which left me between them.

The next level was not open space like most of the first and second floors. Instead we found ourselves in a wide central corridor with three doors on either side, each presumably having a small room beyond it. At the end of the corridor we found the next set of stairs. I thought it unusual that each landing was on the opposite side of the building from that on the floor below.

At the top of these stairs we found a corridor with a layout similar to the one on the third floor.

'Where to?' mouthed Pepper to Martin.

Martin shrugged. And so, because he didn't know, we did the obvious thing and started with the first door on the left.

The room was lined with filing cabinets, and by the window there was a large wooden desk, which I assumed was Mr Levy's. There was a framed photograph of a woman and four children hung on the wall beside the desk.

'Levy's wife?' I said.

Martin shrugged again. It was shocking to realise that

none of us knew that much about Levy or his life outside of Tiffany's, and I admit that I hadn't given it that much thought.

We looked around the room, more out of curiosity than from anything else. On the desk were some papers, letters, bills and payroll information.

Pepper and Martin glanced around and were ready to move on to the next room when we heard the scraping again. This time we knew it was very close by.

'I think you should stay here,' Pepper told me.

'No chance. I'm coming with you,' I said.

We moved down the hall. On this level there were no carpets, so we were walking on polished floorboards only. I tested the stability of each before I stepped on it.

The next door along revealed a room that was dedicated to storage. There were three large safes fitted into it, and I suspected these contained the most valuable diamonds that Martin got to work with only occasionally – if ever. Martin looked at the safes for a moment. His face was serious and it was difficult to know what he was thinking, but I guessed that he might be curious about the contents. The scraping noise was coming from behind the third door. Pepper shifted his cane to his left hand and reached for the handle with his right. Then he pushed the door open.

The sight that greeted us will stay with me for a long time.

The room was in near darkness, lit only by the light we

had brought in with us from the corridor. For a moment I couldn't make sense of the mess.

Edward was hanging upside down from the ceiling. His hair was drooping towards the floor. His normally neat uniform was in a state of disarray. His eyes were wide and bulging, his mouth was slack and open, and red rivulets of blood dripped over his cheeks and down into his hair. Set on the floor beneath him was a large bucket. I could see the blood dripping down into it, forming a deep red pool.

'Edward?' I said, but Edward was no longer in a position to answer me.

His throat had been cut. The scraping noise continued, and it was coming from the shadows at the back of the room. I stared into the gloom and found Levy staring back at me. His eyes were as black as coals but still they glowed in that awful, inhuman way of the zombies. He was holding a razor and leather strap and the scraping we had heard came from his precise movements as he stropped the razor on the leather.

'I'm so hungry. I *challish* for it. But it has to be *kosher*,' said Levy.

'What have you done?' I whispered.

My eyes adjusted to the dim light and I saw that the room was splattered in drips of blood, which I presumed had come from Edward's initial struggle as Levy had cut his throat. The image of the murder wouldn't leave my mind, and I cursed my imagination again for being just too wild, too vivid.

Levy moved out of the shadows and advanced as Pepper and Martin automatically moved in front of me.

'You're a nice girl, Kat. I always liked you. But you're a little too curious for your own good.'

Levy paused. He glared at the two men as though they were punishing him for something he couldn't control. 'I don't want to hurt her,' he said to them, 'but I'm so hungry.'

Martin pushed me back towards the door as Pepper raised his cane in both hands, and before I knew what was happening he had pulled it apart to reveal a sword hidden inside. It gleamed, and I was reminded of Martin's own sword that had been sharpened by the dialight.

Levy laughed at the sight of the sword. Then his face changed, becoming a mask of fury, and he dived at Pepper, swinging the razor before him like a crazed street thug.

Levy was clumsy, unlike Pepper, who had obviously spent some time learning to fence. Pepper moved backwards in a kind of balanced V-step that helped him avoid Levy's weapon while keeping him light on his feet. I noted that his movements were almost dance-like. Smooth and graceful. He didn't appear to be hindered at all by the injury he had sustained in the war.

As Levy threw himself forward, Pepper dodged him again and again. Levy tumbled back into the room, falling against a filing cabinet in the corner and hitting the bucket in the middle with his foot. The blood inside swayed with the impact and splashed out onto the floor, narrowly missing my shoes and the hem of my skirt.

Pepper swung the sword over his head and swirled it in the air as though in some kind of ritual dance. But Levy threw himself aside just as the sword glanced against the cabinet.

Levy was on his feet, arms outstretched as he ran at Pepper once more. His mouth was foaming white like a rabid wolf, and his teeth gnashed at his lips until black blood burst from his mouth.

'I'm hungry!' he roared as though this excused everything.

The sword cut through the air. It connected with Levy's throat, slicing through with barely any difficulty, and Levy's head bounced across the floor and came to rest against the bucket.

It took me a minute to take in that Pepper had decapitated my boss.

'*What*?' Levy's head said with a croak. 'I can't eat regular meat. It's against my religion. You trying to make me break *kashrus*?'

I felt a scream brewing in my throat but I choked it down. This was so horrible. Levy, incredibly, was still alive, even as his body crumpled uselessly to the ground.

'Martin. My boy. Tell them already. I *have* to *kosher* my food.'

He was vile, and this whole thing was monstrous.

Beside me, Martin and Pepper were shocked into silence, but I acted on instinct as the foul creature on the floor began to cackle. I raised the handgun, flipped off the safety, aimed it at Levy's head and fired. A burst of bullets ripped holes in a trail along the floor, then landed in Levy's face before erupting from the back of his head into the metal bucket. His mouth and nose exploded and the bucket was peppered with diamond shards.

I stopped firing. Levy was quiet. Dead for real this time. And I was massively relieved, but so horrified that I couldn't speak.

The room fell silent apart from the slow drip of blood into the bucket from poor Edward.

'I'm proud of you, Kat,' said Pepper. 'That must have been so hard for you.'

'I had to shut him up,' I said. Pepper put his arm around my shoulders and took the gun from my hand, pressed the safety and holstered it again. I stood still and let him take care of me, but the moment of vulnerability passed.

'D ... Does this mean that Edward is one of them?' Martin said.

Pepper looked at Edward and shook his head.

'In his own perverse way, Levy spared him that fate by killing him first.'

The shop girls were screaming and holding each other in panic when the three of us came downstairs. We didn't tell them what had happened, and Martin had taken Levy's key's from his body, locking the door to the room behind us, because we didn't know what else to do with the bodies at that time.

'We could throw them out of the window on the second floor,' Pepper had suggested.

'Feed them to those things? No. We just can't,' I said. And thankfully Martin agreed.

Pepper took Rocky and Danny aside and told them about Levy. I was in a state of shock but I forced myself to go and find Sylvia, because I knew I had to be the one to explain what had happened to Levy. He had been her lover and I was her friend. It was only right that it came from me.

She was hunched up in the corner of the stockroom when I came in. Her arms wrapped around her body.

'Levy's dead,' she said.

'How did you know?'

She looked up at me. 'I went to find him. I wanted to tell him about Judd. I thought he deserved the truth.'

She held out her arm. I saw a wide cut on her wrist, with what appeared to be teeth marks. 'He bit me. Then he sent me away, saying he couldn't see me anymore because I'm not Jewish. I don't understand what's happening.'

I closed my eyes. Fear for her coursing through my already buzzing blood. Sylvia had been bitten. She was going to turn into one of them. Just like Levy.

'What's happening?' asked Pepper coming into the

stockroom behind me. His sword was now sheathed and he was holding the cane as he always did, just like a fashion accessory. But I couldn't get the image from my mind of him turning with a swordsman's skill, the dim light glinting off the blade as it cut cleanly through Levy's neck.

'Martin sharpened your sword with the dialight,' I commented.

'Yes. Indeed he did. I didn't expect it to come in handy so soon.'

I looked at Sylvia. I didn't want to betray her, because I believed that Pepper would probably draw his sword again. I looked away from Pepper and back at Sylvia. Then the decision was taken completely from my hands.

'I'm staying behind tomorrow,' Sylvia said, holding out her arm.

'*Fuck*,' whispered Pepper. 'Pardon me, Miss. I'm so sorry, Ma'am.'

Fifteen

Pepper sat with me behind the counter. I didn't want to be alone and I felt safer with him than with anyone else in the shop.

'It's a deep bite. How long do you think it will take for her to change?'

'It took Levy a few days … But his injury was less direct. I suppose it depends on how long the poison takes to get around the body.'

'This is so awful. She's going to die and there's nothing we can do to help her.'

Pepper sighed and placed his arm around my shoulders. I allowed it because I needed comfort. This could be our last night on Earth and there seemed little point in being obsessed with propriety.

I closed my eyes and tried to imagine Sally and Mother safe in our house with Holly the cat. The little animal had given me so much comfort during the days before the siege.

'I wish my cat was here,' I said.

Pepper sighed again. 'So do I. But at least she'll keep them away from your family.'

'What do you mean? What can a cat do?'

Pepper sighed once more. 'I haven't told you everything,' he admitted. 'I'm sorry. I should have. But I've been trying to make sense of it all myself.'

I looked at Pepper and smiled. 'Tell me now,' I said.

Then Pepper told me the strange story of his journey home in the sick wagons that carried the war wounded back to civilisation.

'I thought I'd left the horrors of the darkness behind in the swamps,' he began. 'And as I travelled back north my mind began to categorise all that I had seen as related to stress. The dead couldn't rise up; we must have buried them prematurely. The men had caught some swamp fever that made them crazy. All of these excuses and more went through my mind until I actually began to believe them.

'None of the other wounded men discussed what had happened. I didn't broach the subject with them, because I feared it was all in my mind. I wanted to put it all down to a bad dream. Or maybe believe that I had suffered from some kind of fever myself that had caused me to hallucinate the whole thing. Whatever had happened, it was all behind me. I was going home and away from the war. Away from death. Away from the darkness that consumed those whose souls were so empty that they needed to be filled by something else.

'We camped along the Mississippi and I was tense, remembering how many good men had been lost there. But there was no sense of the thing I now called the darkness. I considered how it might have moved on with the troops and we were travelling in the opposite direction. That was, until we found Paulson.

'Paulson was catatonic. He couldn't speak, and it was clear he had been living rough in the woods since the day we lost him. The medics examined him and diagnosed a complete mental breakdown, and he was added to the men in the wagons to return home. As the journey commenced, Paulson just lay on his stretcher, never speaking. The medics had to feed him water, which he dutifully drank, but he refused all food, keeping his mouth closed whenever he was offered it. I thought this was strange. By then my internal alarms were starting to go off, because I knew Paulson could be one of *them*.

'I asked the doctor if Paulson had any wounds, and he told me all he could find was a scratch on his wrist. It looked like a cat claw or something like that.

'Then, as we approached the next big city, Paulson began to come out of his stupor. He started to eat again and gradually his foggy expression cleared. "What happened to you?" I asked him eventually. "You just disappeared."

'Paulson turned to me, and his face was blank, like someone who was talking in their sleep. "I went through the dark and couldn't see. Then this happened." He held up his arm. I saw the scratch, just above his wrist. "Cat saved me. He brought me back. And I'll tell you, Pepper, it was hell in the darkness. It was pain, and hunger and sick, sick desires."

'Paulson fell asleep then and when he woke up the next morning he was as good as new. I mulled over what he had said and tried to talk to him again about the darkness, but he refused to revisit that hell, and I can't say that I blamed him. I believe that a cat did save him. And, I think, if we can persuade Sylvia to come with us tomorrow, she may have a chance if we get her back to your house, and to your own cat, Holly.'

'It's worth a try,' I said, letting his latest revelation sink into my brain. 'Let me go and talk to her. I'll tell her what you said and see if she can be persuaded.'

Sylvia was asleep when I looked into the storage room, so I left her and came back to sit with Mr Pepper.

'Tomorrow's the big day,' I said. Then I promptly fell asleep against his shoulder.

We were woken by an unintelligible chanting. It was like a wall of sound surrounding the building. A lullaby that was half remembered. A cry in the night. The images that the noise conjured up in my mind were all of the strangest and most primal ones that I think I could have imagined. I saw the dark forests around the Mississippi, even though I had never been there. I imagined pulling myself up from a cold, dark grave, deep in the swamp. I felt the cold land around me as I marched through the night. It made the starvation sickness in my stomach ache even more.

Pepper twitched beside me and, as I opened my eyes, I realised that he had fallen asleep with me. I crawled away from him as he stretched and moved. I looked out from behind the counter to see Marlene and Rocky ready to go.

'More bullets,' said Martin as he came in with the workshop girls in tow. Lizzie and Agnes helped him pass the ammunition out, and he came over and opened up the tank that was still on my back. He refilled the conveyor, then wound the mechanism as tight as it would go. 'You're good,' he said with a smile.

'Where's Sylvia?' asked Agnes, and I nodded towards the storeroom.

'I'll wake her,' I said.

I went into the storeroom to find Sylvia with her hands over her ears.

'What's wrong?' I asked.

'They are in my head. I can't stop the sound.' I realised then that the zombies were still chanting, but somehow I had zoned them out. 'They know what you're planning to do. You'll never escape. Better to just give into the darkness. I know it's touched you Kat. It's reached us all now.'

'No, Sylvia. We aren't going to give in and neither are you. You're coming with us. Okay?'

Sylvia looked at me. 'I'm becoming one of them, I can feel it.'

'Then fight it. There might be a cure.'

Sylvia was surprised by this, but I didn't elaborate. She pulled herself up and began to straighten her hair and uniform as though she had just realised we were going out into the world and she didn't want to be seen looking untidy.

'We can expect them to attack us. But what I was wondering was, why don't they attack each other?' Marlene was asking Pepper as we came into the sales room.

'Darkness,' said Sylvia. 'They all have it.'

'But they eat their dead,' Rocky said.

'The darkness can't stay in the truly dead.'

Marlene frowned and looked Sylvia over. 'She ain't looking too good.'

'She's going to be fine,' I said, and I smiled and nodded encouragingly at Sylvia. 'We're all looking rough, if the truth be known.'

The plan was simple. We would go through the front door and run right through the crowd while blasting them as much as possible. We hoped that this would distract those around the bodies enough to help us make our escape. It was basic but it could work.

'We need a direction plan. Where we want to end up once we leave the zombies behind,' Pepper pointed out.

'I know a food store nearby. If we can reach it unchallenged they have wagons we can hitch up that we can use to get out of here,' said Rocky. 'That is, unless someone else has beat us to it. But the location is as good as any.'

Danny came in from the back. 'All secure at the back, boss. We ready?'

I had Levy's keys, so I opened the front door and unlocked the grille. The dead stopped chanting and silently stared at us.

'This dialight should work now, right Martin?' Rocky asked, switching his handgun to the diamond light setting.

Martin nodded. His face was pale. He was afraid like the rest of us.

'I should go first,' I said, drawing the Remington. 'This is the fastest and most effective weapon we have.'

'Nah, let's see what this thing can do to these freaks,' said Rocky.

As planned, we lined up. Armed men and women on the outside, workshop girls on the inside. Pepper drew his sword from his cane. 'Aim for the brain,' he said. And then we were off.

Rocky fired first. A beam of sizzling light burnt a neat hole through the head and brain of the nearest zombie, and it crumpled to the ground. I released the safety on my gun and fired a loose arc of bullets into the crowd. The front row exploded in a wet, red and sticky mess of brains, teeth, eyes and skull. Rocky began picking off creatures behind them. To our surprise, the zombies around them stayed where they were. They didn't fall upon the dead and begin to eat as we had expected they would. This was something that was pivotal to our escape. Instead they began to shuffle closer to the shop again, stepping over their fallen members.

'Get back inside,' Pepper said. 'They aren't going for it!'

I slammed the grille closed just as the zombies reached us, but my fingers couldn't work the bolts and locks quickly enough and the grille was tugged and yanked from my hands. I pulled the Remington again and sent a burst of bullets through the metalwork into the close-range faces. Their violent, hungry smiles exploded sickeningly. Blood splashed over the grille and onto my fingers. Rocky pulled me back and we slammed the inner door. By then the zombies were pushing and shoving each other in their battle to get into the small porch that led to the front door. The first of them fell against it and we could tell that there was no way this door would hold for long against the sheer weight of them all pressed in there.

The glass gave first and the zombies at the front reached in, snatching at us with ragged hands and blackened, broken nails. The groom from the first day was at the front and his face was rage-filled. A sickening stench poured into the room. The bodies of the zombies, though seemingly alive, were nonetheless rotting, and they smelt of the foulest of graves.

'Upstairs! Quick,' shouted Martin.

I shot again. The groom took the brunt of the bullets as he was halfway through the glass panel. He twitched and shuddered as the diamonds did their work, but then his body was pulled back and tossed unceremoniously out of the way as more of the creatures pressed forward.

Rocky's dialight stopped working as the room suddenly became starved of natural daylight.

'Shit,' he said, switching back to the bullet setting. Pepper swung his sword and severed the arm of one of the more enterprising creatures who was trying to reach the lock and open the door. Then the door gave way, bursting open under the sheer weight of them. Martin grabbed my arm and pulled me back through and out into the corridor.

Marlene was screaming. Her rifle was snatched from her hands as a zombie grabbed her hair and pulled her violently towards him. I tried to turn back, but Martin was pulling me so hard that my arm was almost wrenched from its socket. I saw Pepper swing his sword at Marlene's assailant, but not before the creature had his hideously rotted mouth around her throat. Her cry was cut off as Pepper swung, burying his sword in the neck of the monster.

Marlene fell down and the zombie's severed head

continued to chew at her even though its body was a useless and crumpled mess beside her.

Rocky placed the barrel of his gun against the head and fired. Then he dropped to his knees beside Marlene. Her eyes were wide open and the severed artery in her neck was still pumping blood, but it was clear she was dead.

'Marlene,' he cried, kneeling beside her as he continued to fire at the zombies now coming easily through the front door.

'Hello lover,' she said.

Then Marlene threw her arms around the big man and bit down hard into his huge stomach. Rocky screamed, and I saw no more as Pepper ran back towards the inner door and we slammed it shut behind us. Pepper quickly ran the security bolts across. The inner door was sturdier than the front door for many reasons. The front door had been designed to look attractive, with a glass panel, and of course it always relied on the grille as extra security. This door was designed to prevent a burglary from the rear of the shop.

'This should hold for a while,' Martin said.

'Where are the girls?' I asked, looking around.

'I sent them upstairs. There are a lot of rooms that are secure there that we can use.'

I nodded. Then I realised that I had dropped Levy's keys at the front door.

'We can't open any of those doors, Martin. I dropped

the keys.'

'Don't worry, I have this one.' Martin held up a strange-looking metal stalk that had a few fine points in various places. 'I can open any lock with this. It's what they call a skeleton key.'

We heard the dead pounding on the door beside us. 'Come on. Let's get upstairs and see how secure we can make this place,' said Pepper.

We backed away to the stairwell and found Danny poised at the top, gun pointed downwards. When he saw it was us, he pointed the gun up to the ceiling and waited for us to come upstairs before he took up point again.

'Danny, I'm so sorry. Mr Spinetti and Marlene …' I said.

Danny nodded but said nothing. He remained a man of few words even in adversity.

Sixteen

We discovered a locked door at the very top of the stairs leading to the fourth floor.

'The more doors we put between us the better,' Martin said, opening the door with his key.

'That's true,' said Sylvia. 'They don't have a huge attention span. They may even forget we're here if they don't find us on the floors they expect to.'

I didn't ask how she knew this, but I remembered how the dead had stubbornly remained outside Tiffany's waiting for us for days. We were like a ripening meal for them and they had shown great endurance in their persistence in wanting to eat it. Even to the point of ignoring the dead whose flesh had previously appealed to them so much.

I said nothing of my thoughts though. I just followed Martin quietly along the corridor until we reached the next stairwell. This too was covered by a locked door. Martin opened it and we herded the girls inside, leaving Pepper and Danny to bring up the rear.

At the top of the stairs there was yet another locked door.

'Good. That will put two more doors and a staircase between us and them if they make it this far. It's a good defensive position,' said Pepper.

Martin opened the door to the fifth and top floor and stepped through. I walked in behind him and stopped dead. The room was a large loft-space that must have taken up most of the roof area. But what made my eyes open wide was what was standing in the centre of the room.

'What is it?' asked Sylvia, coming in behind me.

'A hot air balloon?' said Danny.

The fifth floor ceiling was covered by a glass dome, and a large balloon sat directly underneath it.

It was bullet shaped and made of coarse canvas, with rope laces sewn into the fabric that hung down below it. The ropes were attached to a large wicker basket. Just like a hot air balloon, there were sandbags draped on the sides. The balloon was held in place by several mooring ropes. On the rear of the balloon was a large propeller and just underneath, eye-level if you were standing in the basket, was a wooden box covered in switches and dials. There were two copper pipes that led from the box and into the balloon.

'That's not hot air in there,' Pepper observed, 'otherwise it would be open at the bottom. Besides, the hot air is created by burning a fire beneath it. There is no-one here to maintain something like that.'

Pepper was right. The canvas balloon was completely closed.

'This is our passage out of here,' said Martin, who had been silent up until now.

He ran across the large room and began to turn a crank on the far wall. The dome began to inch open above us, but then Martin closed it again.

'This is meant to go out this way,' he explained.

'Martin, did you create this?' Pepper asked.

'Oh no. Otherwise I would have mentioned it sooner. This is one of my father's creations. Herr Doktor always wanted to make the ultimate flying machine. I didn't know it was here. I have, however, seen his plans for this model. Though I never knew he had actually made it. It's filled with some sort of gas that keeps it erect and lighter than air.'

'Where is your father now?' I asked.

'Dead.'

'I'm sorry,' I said.

'Don't be. When he died, he told me he had left me a legacy. All I had was the skeleton key, but never knew what I would find if I used it. I wish I had realised the airship was here earlier.'

'Airship?' I asked.

'Yes, Kat. This thing can really fly,' Martin said.

'Then let's get out of here,' Agnes said. 'Those things could find us at any time.'

Martin looked around the huge attic space.

'I wonder why Levy kept this a secret from me?'

'How does it work, Martin?' I asked. 'And can we go *now* please?'

We heard a crash below. The eerie chanting echoed up through the floorboards. 'Martin. Martin. Martin.'

'Why are they calling your name?' Pepper asked.

'Because they know he can save you,' said Sylvia.

Her eyes had changed colour. They were paler somehow, like the eyes of the elderly. Watery and weak. And her skin had turned an awful yellow colour.

'No. Sylvia. Not you. We can save you. Fight this!'

'I can't see,' she said. 'It's so dark. There's this cloud around my head and its suffocating me, Kat.'

Then she began to smile that horrible, sick smile that the dead all seemed to share. 'I can see your airship. So they can see it too. You can't escape us, though. The darkness is everywhere. It's spreading down every street, in every town.'

Danny hit her on the back of the neck with the butt of his gun and Sylvia collapsed in a heap, unconscious at our feet.

'I don't wanna kill her,' he said. 'Not if there's a chance that she can be saved.' He glanced at Pepper. 'I heard you tell Miss Lightfoot about the cat last night. If there's a chance, then we should try to save at least one person.'

'Eloquently put, Danny,' said Pepper. 'Martin, is there anything we can use to tie her up? The last thing we need is her waking when we're up in the air.'

Martin looked around the room and came back with a small coil of cord or rope. I looked away as they tied Sylvia's arms and legs and placed a gag between her teeth too. 'We don't need her biting anyone else,' Pepper explained when he saw my distaste.

'Will this carry us all?' I asked, looking at the workshop girls. Lizzie, Agnes, Hermione, Maude, Emily and June were gathered around the airship, looking out of the huge window and over the city. There were ten of us left out of the original 15 people who had been trapped inside Tiffany's. We had to all fit in the basket, and the airship had to carry us all. It was essential that we didn't lose anyone else.

'I don't know,' said Martin finally. 'But I think it's okay.'

'How does this thing fly, then?' asked Pepper.

'I'm not too sure, but if you give me an hour I'll try to figure it out.'

Unfortunately we didn't have an hour.

There was a crash as one of the lower doors gave way. We could hear the dead now, down the stairs on the fourth floor, and they were heading our way. This was the time to truly test the theory that the stairway was defensible.

'Climb in the basket,' Martin shouted, and everyone

moved at once.

Martin went to the handle and started to crank open the dome. Danny and Pepper lifted the prone body of Sylvia in, and the workshop girls helped each other over the edge of the basket. Then Pepper and Danny went back to the door and stared down the staircase.

There was a further crash as the door at the bottom was smashed in.

'They're coming!' shouted Danny, and he and Pepper opened fire at the creatures as they stumbled into the stairway and up the final flight of stairs.

Martin had fully opened the dome now, and he jumped into the basket and started to study the control panel.

'Kat, get in yourself!' shouted Pepper. 'You need to be ready to go when Martin figures out how it works.'

'I'm not leaving you. Let me use the Remington on them.'

Danny fired down, but had to stop frequently to reload. I used this time to switch places with him and fired several spurts of diamond shard bullets into the zombie mob. They fell, but then, just as downstairs, the others came past them, heaving their bodies up and over their own heads and out of the way while continuing to come up the stairs. It was like an unending siege of insects. No matter how quickly you killed them, more came to take their place. And the frightening thing was, they weren't completely mindless: they had an agenda and they were working together to achieve it.

'I think I have it,' Martin shouted.

I heard a loud stuttering burst of noise, like grinding clockwork parts, all moving together in the wrong way. A loud ticking noise came from the ship, and a long drawn-out hiss erupted from the copper pipes.

The zombies below became enraged and began to come even faster up the stairwell. Danny took up point again and fired rapidly into the space, while I sent the bullets pouring down unchecked.

More bodies were hefted out of the way, followed by more of the zombies. Then the Remington stopped working. I tried it several times, but it was jammed.

'It's not working,' I yelled over Danny's gunfire.

'Get into the basket,' Pepper shouted and then he and Danny slammed the top door shut and secured the bolts on it. 'Martin, how are we doing?'

'Getting there,' said Martin.

'I thought you had it already?'

'I'm working out how to drive it. It's not like a horse!'

'This door isn't going to hold for very long,' Danny said, keeping his full weight against it. 'Mr Pepper, please make sure that the ladies are safe. Get into the airship yourself.'

'I've got it,' Martin said.

I threw myself into the basket as it leapt up slightly, tugging against the mooring ropes. Then I shrugged the tank off my back and opened it. The bullet conveyor was twisted and had somehow managed to stop the mechanism from spinning. I reached in and turned the belt, straightening it out until the runner was correctly aligned. There were only a dozen or so bullets left inside, so I pulled some more from my pocket and began to reload the magazine. I managed to get ten more bullets in before Agnes screamed and I knew we had finally run out of time.

I stood up in the basket as the door burst open. Poor Danny was buried in lumps of wood and staggering zombies. Pepper leaped back and dashed for the basket. I slammed the tank shut, lifted the gun and squeezed the trigger just as Pepper reached us.

The gun failed again. I went into a panic. What had I done wrong? Then I remembered that I hadn't rewound the mechanism. I gave the key a few turns, aimed and fired, and the rain of bullets knocked the first wave of zombies right back down the stairs.

The basket began to lift, then halted.

'What is it?' asked Pepper.

'Mooring ropes,' I said, firing the gun again. I was trying to count the bullet bursts but it was too difficult to do.

Pepper pulled the sword from his cane and swung hard at the ropes. The first one cut with the first stroke but he had to climb over the girls in order to reach the second rope. All of which gave the creatures time to enter the chamber.

The airship lifted up shakily as the final rope was severed, then halted again.

'We're too heavy,' yelled Martin.

Pepper began to cut at the ropes holding the sandbags to the side of the basket. One and then two fell free and thumped to the floor below. We lifted a few feet higher, and the balloon was almost out of the dome, but then it halted again.

The zombies were below us now. Their arms were waving and they were roaring with frustration.

Pepper cut away another sandbag, and another. The bags hit the creatures below us, but this seemed to make no difference to them. The ship rose higher and suddenly we were flying clear of the dome and up above the building.

I laughed out loud in relief at the angry mob below. Their fury was suddenly ludicrous, and then I was slumped on the floor of the basket, crying and laughing.

I pulled myself together when I saw that Hermione was gently wiping Sylvia's face with a handkerchief.

'She hasn't woken up yet,' said the girl calmly.

When did this happen?, I found myself wondering. *How did they all get to be so brave?*

'Well done!' said Pepper to me, sheathing his sword once more. 'You're a brave girl and no mistake.'

'We are all brave,' I said, looking around.

'Look at this,' Martin said. I stood up and looked out over New York. 'Down below.'

I looked down, experienced a brief burst of vertigo, and then saw what Martin was indicating.

'What the devil is that?' asked Pepper.

I squinted. We were far above the building now, perhaps by another five floors. All I could see were some fast, colourful blurs moving in and out of the swarming horde of zombies.

'Can you lower us?' I asked, and Martin nodded, turning back to the dials.

He made some minor adjustments and, with a hiss of releasing gas, the airship began slowly to descend. I watched the ground get nearer until I could make sense of what I was seeing.

'That's enough,' I said, and the airship came to a jerky halt around 30 feet above the ground.

It all began to make sense. The blurs of colour became subtle patterns and, on closer inspection, shiny fur. The neighbourhood cats had joined the fight.

As I watched I saw one cat launch itself from a tree and land on the head of one of the zombies that was coming back out of Tiffany's. The cat, a ginger tom, dug his claws into the creature's scalp and jumped away, like a flea abandoning a rat, onto another one, as the first zombie fell to the floor.

The creatures, once scratched by the cats, tumbled to the ground and lay there unmoving.

'Will they recover?' I wondered as more cats appeared, streaming over and onto the zombies. They scratched and bit until all of the zombies fell.

'I doubt it,' said Pepper. 'I think these were long dead anyway. Perhaps the ones like Sylvia, half turned, still have a chance.'

We hovered over Fifth Avenue until we saw no more movement below and then Martin turned the airship away and we headed across town towards my street. As we travelled I saw the dead falling as the city was overrun once more – not by the zombies this time, but by our seemingly harmless pets.

Epilogue

The row of town houses looked just as they had when I had left home days before. The only difference now was the pile of bodies that lay strewn in the street. There was no movement from within the houses, and Martin was worried about landing the ship in case an attack came quickly from one of them.

Instead he dropped a rope ladder over the side for Pepper and me, and we climbed down onto the rungs, jumping to ground just outside my home.

During the flight I had reloaded my gun – and wound the mechanism – and Pepper still held onto his trusty walking stick, but now had another loaded gun in his pocket should he need it.

I tried my key in the door but found that the security chain was on from the inside. 'Mother!' I yelled through the gap. 'It's me! Are you and Sally all right?'

I heard a meow and Holly bounded towards the door.

'Kat? Is that really you?' Mother was right behind the cat.

'Yes Mother, and Mr Pepper is with me. We escaped from Tiffany's.'

She released the chain and opened the door and Holly leaped up my body and into my arms, meowing so loudly that it felt like she was telling me everything they had been through.

'Are you okay?' I asked, throwing my free arm around Mother.

'Yes, but it was touch and go for Sally for a while. She was playing in the yard and her friend Katie came in and bit her. I always disliked that girl. Strange behaviour to go around biting people.'

I learnt that Mother and Sally had been fighting their own battle, and thanks to Holly, both Katie and Sally were now recovering from their brief skirmish with the darkness. Holly had appeared in the yard, bitten Katie and scratched Sally.

'They both fell into this deep sleep,' Mother said. 'Then this morning Sally woke up and was racing around as if nothing had happened. Soon afterwards Katie was asking for hot milk.'

Outside, the neighbours were slowly coming out of their houses to look in amazement at the airship.

Mr Pepper was standing by the door, keeping an eye out, and Mrs Handley hailed him. 'Oh Mr Pepper. This is my son James, come home on leave.'

Pepper went to the front gate and shook hands with the soldier. They exchanged a few words that made me realise that not all of the soldiers had been touched by the sickness.

'This has been the strangest few days,' said James Handley. 'I almost want to go back to camp for a rest.'

Pepper nodded.

I walked out of my house and looked up at the airship, Holly still snuggled in my arms. She sniffed the air and mewed, and I hoped it wouldn't be too late for Sylvia. She didn't deserve the lot she had been served, but then who did?

Martin lowered the airship down, finally feeling secure that the dead were not going to rise again.

I looked out at my quiet street and, as I saw more normal people emerge from their houses, followed by their cats, I wondered if New York would ever recover from this pestilence.

'It will be a slow and difficult process, but we have the cats to help us prevent resurgence,' I heard Pepper say. 'There's just one question that keeps on going around in my head. Why did the cats take so long to get to us?'

I looked around at the dead bodies in the street, and recalled the devastation in all of the city blocks that the airship had travelled over.

'It's obvious really,' I said. 'They were busy clearing *all* of the streets.'

I snuggled the cat in my arms. 'I still don't know how you got into the safe,' I whispered. Holly purred and meowed as though the solution was perfectly clear. That was a question to which I would probably never have an answer, but I did know one thing. Call it intuition, or maybe on some level Holly communicated her intent to me. I wasn't sure. But I was completely certain about this: the cats had *always* known about the darkness.

I wondered if this was why they could often be seen patrolling at night. Maybe they were holding back this evil that tried to sneak up on man when he was at his weakest. But then, maybe those thoughts were for another time. For now, we had survived, and I knew that whatever fight came my way in the future, I would be ready for it.

Yiddish Words and Phrases Used in This Book

Meshugginas	A mad person/nutter
Oy-yoy-yoy	A joyous or sarcastic exclamation
Oy gevalt	How terrible
Schmuck	An idiot; strong word for a penis; basically calling someone a jerk or prick
Shlepper	A layabout/an untidy person with no aim in life
Gonif	Usually means thief, but can refer to someone who is untrustworthy
Chutzpah	Cheek; example would be a shoplifter who brought back what they stole for a refund
Machen a gevalt	Cause a scene or yell for help
Oy vey	A shocked exclamation, like saying 'Oh, no!'
Dreck	A vulgar expression liking saying something or someone is 'shit' or 'ugly'
Challish	Starving or hungry
Kosher	Food that has been killed and prepared by Jewish law; blessed by a Rabbi
Kashrus	The laws that Jews must follow with regards to diet

About the Author

Award winning author Sam Stone began writing aged 11 after reading her first adult fiction book, *The Collector* by John Fowles. Her love of horror fiction began soon afterwards when she stayed up late one night with her sister to watch Christopher Lee in the classic Hammer film, *Dracula*. Since then she's been a huge fan of vampire movies and novels old and new.

Sam's writing has appeared in nine anthologies for poetry and prose. Her first novel was the fulfilment of a lifelong dream. Like all good authors she drew on her own knowledge and passions to write it. The novel won the Silver Award for Best Horror Novel in *ForeWord* Magazine's book of the year awards in 2007.

In September 2008 the novel was re-edited and republished by The House of Murky Depths as *Killing Kiss*. The sequels, *Futile Flame* and *Demon Dance* went on to become finalists in the same awards for 2009/2010. Both novels were later Shortlisted for The British Fantasy Society Awards for Best Novel and *Demon Dance* won the award for Best Novel in 2011. Sam also won Best Short Fiction for her story *Fool's Gold* which first appeared in the NewCon Press Anthology *The Bitten Word.*

An eclectic and skilled prose writer Sam also has a BA (Hons) in English and Writing for Performance and an MA in Creative Writing, which means that she is frequently invited to talk about writing in schools, colleges and universities in the UK. She is said to be an 'inspirational' speaker.

Zombies in New York and Other Bloody Jottings
by Sam Stone

Something is sapping the energy of the usually robust dancers of the Moulin Rouge … Zombies roam the streets of New York City … Clowns die in mysteriously humorous ways … Jack the Ripper's crimes are investigated by a vampire …

Welcome to the horrific and poetic world of Sam Stone, where Angels are stalking the undead and a vampire becomes obsessed with a centuries-old werewolf. Terror and lust go hand in hand in the disturbing world of the Toymaker, and the haunting Siren's call draws the hapless further into a waking nightmare.

Thirteen stories of horror and passion, and six mythological and erotic poems from the pen of the new Queen of Vampire fiction.

Chick-slash has never been so entertaining

Contains the 2011 British Fantasy Award Winning short story 'Fool's Gold'.

352pp. 'B' format collection.
ISBN 978-1-84583-055-7 (pb)
Paperback £12.99

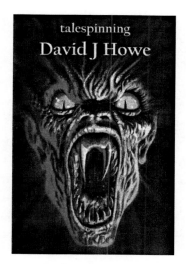

talespinning
by David J Howe

'In front of him, backlit by a faint green glow, a third figure seemed to appear from the motes of dust floating in the air. It took a step towards him, metal instruments clinking gently at its waist. Tony sat staring at the figure. His heart was beating nineteen to the dozen, and, despite the chill air, sweat broke out on his pate and started to run down his temples.'

Horror stalking the streets, druggies after the latest high, fairies in the garden and haunted thrash metal albums ... just some of the bizarre and compelling tales from the talented pen of David J Howe.

Encompassing short stories, screenplays, and extracts from other pieces, talespinning is a fascinating dip into the unknown. If vampires, imaginary dogs, time-travelling ghosts and wishes that come true appeal, then this collection has something for you!

464pp. 'B' format collection.
ISBN 978-1-84583-058-8 (pb)
Paperback £12.99

THE DJINN by Graham Masterton

Anna is mysterious and beautiful, so much so that clairvoyant, Harry Erskine, breaks propriety and asks her out to lunch at his Godfather's wake. When his Godmother, Marjorie Greaves, reveals the strange behaviour of her recently deceased husband, Max, Harry and Anna offer to investigate the strange jar that has been locked away in the turret. Harry soon learns that Anna is not all that she seems, and little can prepare him for the power of the Forty Thieves, the most potent genie in the history of Persia.

Racing against time, Harry, Anna and Professor Qualt must work together to prevent an unexpected enemy from opening the jar and unleashing the ancient and prevailing djinn on an unsuspecting world.

Graham Masterton's terrifying 1977 novel is republished by Telos in a brand new edition, complete with an exclusive introduction by the author.

'Graham Masterton is one of the few true masters of the horror genre.' James Herbert

128pp. A5 reprint paperback novel.
ISBN 978-1-84583-052-6 (pb)
Paperback £9.99

HUMPTY'S BONES by Simon Clark

Telos Publishing is proud to announce the publication of a new horror novella by one of the supreme horror writers working in the UK today. Simon Clark's new chiller explores something nasty found in a village garden by an amateur archaeologist, something which has lain buried for centuries, and which has seen tribute paid to it by generations of local inhabitants. But what happens when the bones are removed and Humpty once more stalks the Earth ...

With an evocative cover by multiple award winning artist Vincent Chong, the book contains HUMPTY'S BONES, a special introduction and author's notes by Simon Clark, and a new long short story called DANGER SIGNS, about a group of children who investigate an abandoned military bunker, and find that everything there is not quite as dead as they expected.

122pp A5 original paperback novella.
ISBN 978-1-84583-051-9 (pb)
Paperback £9.99

OTHER HORROR/FANTASY FROM TELOS

URBAN GOTHIC: LACUNA AND OTHER TRIPS edited by DAVID J
HOWE
Tales of horror from and inspired by the Urban Gothic televison series.
Contributors: Graham Masterton, Christopher Fowler, Simon Clark, Steve
Lockley & Paul Lewis, Paul Finch and Debbie Bennett.
£8.00 (+ £2.50 UK p&p) Standard p/b ISBN: 1-903889-00-6

APPROACHING OMEGA by ERIC BROWN
A colonisation mission to Earth runs into problems.
£7.99 (+ £2.50 UK p&p) Standard p/b ISBN: 1-903889-98-7
£30.00 (+ £2.50 UK p&p) Deluxe signed and numbered h/b
ISBN: 1-903889-99-5

VALLEY OF LIGHTS by STEPHEN GALLAGHER
A cop comes up against a body-hopping murderer.
£9.99 (+ £3.00 UK p&p) Standard p/b ISBN: 1-903889-74-X
£30.00 (+ £3.00 UK p&p) Deluxe signed and numbered h/b
ISBN: 1-903889-75-8

PRETTY YOUNG THINGS by DOMINIC MCDONAGH
A nest of lesbian rave bunny vampires is at large in Manchester. When
Chelsey's ex-boyfriend is taken as food, Chelsey has to get out fast.
£7.99 (+ £2.50 UK p&p) Standard p/b ISBN: 1-84583-045-8

A MANHATTAN GHOST STORY by T M WRIGHT
Do you see ghosts? A classic tale of love and the supernatural.
£9.99 (+ £3.00 UK p&p) Standard p/b ISBN: 1-84583-048-2

SHROUDED BY DARKNESS: TALES OF TERROR edited by ALISON L
R DAVIES
An anthology of tales guaranteed to bring a chill to the spine. This collection
has been published to raise money for DebRA, a national charity working
on behalf of people with the genetic skin blistering condition, Epidermolysis
Bullosa (EB). Featuring stories by: Debbie Bennett, Poppy Z Brite, Simon
Clark, Storm Constantine, Peter Crowther, Alison L R Davies, Paul Finch,
Christopher Fowler, Neil Gaiman, Gary Greenwood, David J Howe, Dawn
Knox, Tim Lebbon, Charles de Lint, Steven Lockley & Paul Lewis, James
Lovegrove, Graham Masterton, Richard Christian Matheson, Justina
Robson, Mark Samuels, Darren Shan and Michael Marshall Smith. With
a frontispiece by Clive Barker and a foreword by Stephen Jones. Deluxe
hardback cover by Simon Marsden.
£12.99 (+ £3.00 UK p&p) Standard p/b ISBN: 1-84583-046-6
£50.00 (+ £3.00 UK p&p) Deluxe signed and numbered h/b
ISBN: 978-1-84583-047-2